PRAISE

AND ESTEVAN VEGA:

"Estevan's writing reminds me of a fever dream. I've said it before, and I'll say it again: Keep an eye on Estevan Vega."

—PJ Carroll, *Lytherus.com*

"*Winter Sparrow* is a twisted fairy tale where the happily ever after is just within reach but instead you are led through a maze of love, loss and betrayal, never quite sure where you are headed or what you want to happen next. Estevan Vega challenges the reader to go deep within their psyche and leaves you with this cautionary thought: Be careful what you wish for."

—Karen, *For What It's Worth Reviews*

"Estevan Vega is a fabulous storyteller. He's highly prolific and young—I can't wait to watch his career roll out; I have a feeling he's going to be a major force in fiction."

—Robert Liparulo, bestselling author of
The 13th Tribe and *The Dreamhouse Kings* series

"Never have I been left thinking about a story for days after reading it as much as I have been with this one. To say that it is beautifully written is an understatement."

—Holly Warner, *Bookworm in Barrie*

FOR VAL,

WINTER is A MOMENT.
LOVE is FOREVER

Winter Sparrow

TRUE. LOVE. FOREVER

ESTEVAN VEGA

2K18

CAPULET
ENTERTAINMENT

CAPULET ENTERTAINMENT

First Paperback Edition: 2012

ISBN: 978-0990537816

Cover Design by Tyler Evans
Edited by Audra Marvin
Interior Design by D. Robert Pease, www.walkingstickbooks.com

OTHER PUBLISHED WORKS:

Arson
Ashes
Arise

The Forsaken

Music Box (short)
The Borrower (short)

When Colors Bleed *(Short Story Collection)*
Baby Blue
Vanilla Red
The Man in the Colored Room

Books published prior to *Arson*:
Servant of the Realm
The Sacred Sin

For the bride

TRUE. LOVE. FOREVER

Spring

1

IT WAS MARY'S FIRST TIME in the country. She'd driven through secluded parts of the state before but never like this. In her youth, she didn't have the chance to linger anywhere long enough for the place to really get to know who she was or for her to be anything more than a passing shadow.

Her father had it set in his mind to expose his children to a diverse life and a number of experiences she now kept tucked away in some deep, dark closet of herself. In spite of his unusual way of loving, it was never Mary's intent to run away like she had. But the *never-looking-back* part came a little too easily. *I have to be free.* That's what she'd said. Thought, actually. The words were never fully conceived. She supposed they lived somewhere inside of her too, with the items she preferred to leave nameless.

She glanced down at the ring on her finger; it told her she had become a skilled actress waiting for a cue to dash onto the stage. Waiting for the crescendo of jeers to label her a phony. But she couldn't be that. She was a bride to be, after all; "the perfect sparrow," as Joshua called her.

Mary pulled her eyes away from the engagement ring for a minute, long enough to study Joshua's profile. Such an effortless piece of art it was. The shadow of the evening sunlight poured in from the windshield and from the blue skies beyond, making his features seem even more magical.

She liked how the hair on his chin graced it just so she'd know it was there. Nothing fancy, nothing pretentious, just simple and handsome. Mary especially liked the pattern his teeth fell into. A mouth had never looked so accurately composed, and without the aid of cruel metal and overpaid professionals. It was a smile that could melt any girl's heart.

Mary didn't realize she had been squeezing Joshua's hand or that cutting off his circulation would cause him to swerve unintentionally. She sank back into her seat, a little embarrassed, mostly thankful they didn't crash.

"Sorry," she eventually said in a hush.

He reached for her hand again nonetheless, after letting the blood return, and kissed it. "It's nothing."

That smile revisited her in the stillness of the sedan. She felt so safe here with him. So known. But it wasn't at all like she had thought it would be. Her love for Joshua wasn't the stuff of fairy tales or high-gloss Hollywood productions; it was deeper.

Then why did it take so long for you to say yes? her mind intruded.

She didn't have a good enough answer. Perhaps it was because this world had left its mark on her somehow. Even though she was young, it was like a year could be a lifetime. She'd fallen behind. Joshua reminded her what it felt like to be alive. She had given up on relationships before meeting him, claiming they were nothing more than an insecure girl's ego trip. A trip she had sworn off.

But oaths could be broken, couldn't they? Couldn't she mask that part of herself that believed love could never really work? She felt sure she could, and she would.

Mary rolled down the window and invited the April breeze to kiss her face. With every blink, the car carried them deeper into the country that she inwardly confessed still made her uneasy. "It's not the place that bothers me," she had told Joshua before agreeing to the Sunday drive. "It's something else." That something else never came out. That something else was still hiding at the back of her tongue.

Buying a home had always been one of those unmentionable things. The scary things couples rarely talked about, like getting pregnant or meeting the in-laws. She wasn't necessarily against owning a home, even though she was already beginning to dread the amount of energy she'd be required by default to dedicate to something that wasn't even alive; the truly scary thing was the implication of the idea itself. She knew what it really meant: She was committed. Truly committed, not just to a man but to a piece of property. In what right world were people ever supposed to commit themselves to bricks and stones?

She inhaled a long, cool drag of wind.

But this wasn't just a home, was it? It didn't even require a down payment from them. Not a signature, not a bribe to the loan clerk at the credit union. It was a gift. Joshua claimed the deed had been in the Clay family for generations. Mary was tempted to try and convince Joshua to sell it before she even laid eyes on it. Something about not wanting to get attached, she would've said. *As if.* The truth was that she doubted it would appeal to her—a secluded structure out in the middle of some serial killer's fantasy? No, thanks. Besides, chances were good that it had a rodent infestation and was crawling with spiders; and surely the walls boasted the heads of wild animals. Or maybe the place was condemned and in need of a good exorcist.

Her ridiculous theories did nothing to settle the anxiety twisting in her stomach. Not like theories ever could. If the medication couldn't settle her, if the therapy she'd endured over the years couldn't settle her, then what would? Not Joshua's kind whispers or his affectionate hand stroking hers. Not even a scenario with a proposed happy ending, because Mary knew happy endings were like half-smiles or half-truths. They were pages left unfinished in books she didn't really want to be a part of, especially when she knew, beneath the façade she had created, that every intruding thought was a cunning politician, and unsure moments like these were when such ugly roots were exhumed.

You're being too harsh of the situation, Mary. If anyone could appreciate beauty, an artist like her could, so it wasn't the fact that it couldn't ever be beautiful out here. Something else. From a young, impressionable age, Mary had been capable of seeing what was beautiful, even if it wasn't always there. Most times she could look at a blank canvas and picture the life about to be created by her meticulous, capricious talents. Of course, Dad didn't think she had it in her to be a painter. In his mind, the pursuit of art as a lifelong ambition was nothing but a romantic dream that could only result in a rude awakening. A consequence of her condition. *After all, so much of an artist's life is loneliness,* he'd said, *and your mind is too fragile for that.* But in spite of her father's attempt to keep her caged, whether he knew or didn't know how his words imprisoned her, she proved him wrong.

Still, judgment and critique did not cease. Dad never thought Joshua was a good enough lover for his complicated offspring either. But he was wrong there as well. *Zero for two, Dad*, she thought, mentally gloating a bit.

But there was a fear growing with the ugly roots. The fear was strong and relentless. Years of feeling in control had led her here, now so lost with who she was and what she wanted, a delirium swimming in her blood that could not be sedated.

"It's going to be beautiful out here, promise," Joshua said, momentarily derailing her train of thought.

Why was it that, when he promised something, he really seemed to mean it? Or at least, she felt able to trust that he meant it. Maybe it was the power each of his words possessed or how he stole a tender glance of her when he spoke the words. Without fail, he had this presence that forced her doubts to be still, if only for a short while. Nothing up until now could calm her, but his words did. Where were these simple words when she was trapped in that filthy high school locker room? Where was he when pompous doctors filled her brain with reasons to be afraid of what she might become as a result of some genetic mistake?

"I met you too late," she said, kissing his wrist and smiling as the gentleness of those micro-hairs tickled her mouth.

"What do you mean?" Joshua asked, one second his eyes glued to the road and the next to her.

"I feel so obsolete sometimes. Outdated."

"You're not old, if that's what you mean."

"No, I'm not. But I feel like my life is passing me by, attempting to leave me...I don't know...incomplete, unfulfilled.

Joshua grinned. "Passing? I was under the impression we were about to *begin* our lives together. Most girls would be on cloud nine."

"And I am. Oh, don't listen to me," she said, brushing off her remark as silliness. "My mind just never knows when to keep its opinions to itself, that's all."

"Are you having second thoughts about the wedding?"

"No."

"About this drive?"

"I don't think so?"

"That sounded more like a question than an answer," he said. "What is it? I'm not gonna force you to do anything you don't wanna do, Mary. I love you." He paused. "Is it my father's house?"

She slowly nodded. "I guess."

"This area will start to feel like home in no time, really. You haven't even seen it yet."

"No, I haven't. But it doesn't mean I can't ever get lost out here and have some grungy perv attempt to take advantage of me. What then?"

Joshua rolled his eyes. "You'd probably give said grungy perv a piece of your mind, and he'd run off with his tail between his legs."

Mary felt her shoulders rise to cradle a chilled neck. She rolled up the window as a slight smirk nudged her lips. "How do you do that?"

"What?" he asked.

"Always make me feel like everything's gonna be all right. Like I'm this beautiful, courageous person."

"Because that's how I see you."

"I wish we saw the same thing. No one's as beautiful as you think I am."

"I've known you for years now. I think I'm a pretty good judge."

"Just wondering if three years is enough time to get to know someone before you rush into something." She didn't realize what was coming out of her mouth until it was too late. It was sort of like vomit. The syllables just kept bubbling up out of her. "I didn't mean...That came out wrong. It's not you."

"We're not rushing, sweetheart. We both have given it a lot of time and thought, and you've wrestled with it, I know. But it just feels like the right move."

Move, like it's a game of chess. How quaint.

Joshua guided the car around the foot of a great hill. She'd noticed the sky change colors during the trip. It started as an inviting fuchsia, but as night fell, the atmosphere became a grayer shade. Each hour brought change. It was the nature of the world. It wasn't a nightmare or a reason to be afraid. It just was. At least, that's what her father might've said if he were here. And the tall trees surrounding this winding road weren't ghastly, looming menaces. They were breathtaking guardians.

A blink. Return to reality.

Maybe that was how she was supposed to think. Maybe these forest mysteries could be easily defined during the daylight. But when the colors shifted into place, when the night dropped out of those moving clouds, everything turned. The sky became less magical. The tress turned into swaying sentinels she had every reason to be afraid of.

The anxiety returned suddenly and drove needles up her forearm. Mary hoped Joshua didn't catch her weighing every breath. She shut her eyes, wishing to be free from the insatiable thoughts. But the gesture didn't help much. The car was still bending her, pulling her toward a certain unknown destination, possibly an end if the numerous statistics she'd perused in several magazines proved correct.

To her fiancé, Mary knew this wasn't anything close to an end. Rather, it was a beginning. A new life. *Maybe my second chance*, she eventually mused, and then she kept that thought spinning in her mind for a while.

2

SHE WOULD NEVER FORGET THE unpleasant feeling of stepping out of the car and walking up to the house her parents had decided was going to be their new home, like it or not. But a home was more than the walls. It was more than a building. It was the people in it.

"Right," Mary had said with rolled eyes before her mother had the chance to finish her rant. The home possessed an aura she hadn't before sensed in any other house. Then again, she'd only ever lived in two houses. She didn't even count their three-month stint in the grungy apartment back in Missouri as living. It was a brief episode she pretended never happened.

Mary was fourteen for a moment. She was so sure of who she was. Or, at least, she was sure of the kind of girl she *wanted* to be. The kind that grows wings and flies into a brighter existence. Maybe she had acquired that trait from her old man. Dad, with his unflinching demeanor and eyes that had more determination than any rugged guy she'd ever day-dreamed about, had been the reason they always moved from place to place. The luxury of being the daughter of a third-class factory worker.

But that's the way things look when you're young. Things happen because they have a *reason* to happen. People do because something pushes them in that direction. A reason. A poem where human beings and the hopeless, romantic mistakes create each miserable stanza. Was it his selfish plan or his ambition that drew them to the house of her teenage years? The house she swore she would hate with every footprint she left behind on the uneven wood floors or for every stroke of her palm against the sloppily painted drywall. Yes, this was who she wanted to be. The girl who had a reason to be frustrated, discontent. Left behind like footprints. Mary knew who she was becoming, even then. But nobody else had a clue.

"I'll grow wings all by myself," she scribbled into the bed frame one night. It was remarkable what one could accomplish with a twisted paperclip and a splinter of light creeping in. Her little sister, Jamie, never even stirred while she scratched and scratched away. "I'll grow wings."

The quiet tap of the rain on her passenger side window brought back the rusted memory. The truth of it was that it did indeed taste like metal, if memories could taste like anything. She remembered seeing a sparrow that day her family transported her to a place far from any home she wanted to think about. Perhaps some of the finer memories were dead, hidden away in that subconscious closet of hers. If a thought were left alone long enough, could it too grow wings and fly away?

Get a grip, Mary. It's just a house, she thought, the realism of these adolescent moments flooding in. *It will be your new home.* She was back in the car with Joshua, knowing full well that it wasn't as simple as giving the place a name. Mary's home or Joshua's home. Or Joshua's father's home. What were possessions anyway, if not things to be given and taken and named? And was that all she was to him? A possession? Something to be had, here and now, to be carried to some distant, secluded house, away from the world she knew she needed to be in?

What, then, was the reason for this drive? Surely she wasn't prepared to walk down the aisle. She didn't have the shoes, the dress, and if any of her family members could see her now, they'd point and laugh. So nervous, hands shaking to a panicked melody, eyes fixed on the darkness that lay behind the tall trees. She hadn't bothered to apply any makeup either, icing on the tasteless cake. All the gook in the world couldn't mask the uncertain glow in her stare.

"What if we didn't see it?" she offered up quietly. Joshua had been listening to the soft music he enjoyed during long car rides. Mozart or Beethoven; she wasn't good at distinguishing between the two.

Her fiancé lowered the volume. "What, baby?

"I said, what if we didn't see the house right now?"

"We drove all this way. It wouldn't make much sense to turn back now. You are acting so strange today." The car kept pulling her closer. Where were her wings? She thought that by now they'd be developed, tugging their feathered way out of her shoulders. Real. Strong. "Mary, don't look so bewildered. We're safe here. I told you, this house has been in my family for generations. My father has given it to me, and I want to give it to you. Don't mind the woods."

"What if I don't want it?" She felt guilty for how those words just dropped off her tongue.

"You'll like it. Trust me."

Trust. Maybe that was why she'd gotten in this car. Maybe that was why she didn't beg him, even now, to slam on the brakes and let her run back, ever waiting for the wings to carry her into the pale clouds and back to the city.

She sat in silence. There weren't any more memories during the car ride. She was thankful for that. Seeing her parents' faces again in her mind's eye had been disconcerting, especially now, when all she really wanted to see was a light amidst so much black.

"We're finally here," Joshua said with excitement nearly an hour later. He couldn't help nudging her lethargic legs a half a dozen times, awaiting her reaction.

The car eased up the small crest and entered a dirt-and-pebble passage that cities and suburbia would never have called a driveway. Joshua stopped in front of the porch. The lawn, or what was supposed to be a lawn, was overgrown with weeds. And there was a tarnished, broken-down tractor that looked to be from her grandfather's day half taken apart and sleeping beside a massive willow tree. Judging by the bumps that sent vibrations through her seat on the slow drive in, she surmised that the rocks and unsympathetic roots were responsible for killing the massive mechanical beast.

The grass and weeds came up to her ankles. Their skinny, wind-tossed bodies scratched her skin. She itched. A pair of fireflies lit up a bit of the night around her cheeks. It was odd that something so small and simple could bring a smile to her face.

Mary heard Joshua's car door slam shut seconds later. He walked through a slush pile of mud and weeds and stood next to her. The goose bumps would settle eventually, she told herself, as she twisted around to try and get a clear view of the property. Blink after blink, Mary's eyes were met with pitch black. All of a sudden, the happy insects were gone, and new darkness seemed to envelop them.

"Home, sweet home," Joshua said with a deep breath. He threw one arm around her shoulder.

Mary shrugged. The enormous house seemed plagued with sadness.

"Shall we go inside?" he said with a creepy whisper.

"Can't wait," she replied, rolling her eyes. She took his hand and walked toward the front door.

It was almost cute seeing her fiancé stumble around for a light switch. She was just glad the place had electricity. *Calm down, Mary. This isn't the house of a pilgrim, for heaven's sake. It's his father's house. He isn't some weirdo.*

At least, not that you know of.

"When my father told me he was giving me the house, I just about flipped. Can you believe this place? It's...well, it's..."

"An albatross?" she said. "Filthy? In the middle of nowhere? Cold?"

"And dark too, and spooky." He couldn't help but make ridiculous faces when he spoke. "And yes, in the middle of nowhere. But it's so much more. I'm surprised you can't see its potential. It's magnificent."

They stepped inside.

How could he call this thing magnificent? Was it the peeling linoleum floor? Or the kitchen cabinets with doors that didn't close the right way? Maybe it was the fact that the ceiling had been dripping water onto the unfinished maple in the lower dining room. As Mary scanned a number of the lower-level rooms, she wondered if she really belonged here or if, like the tractor outside, she'd be pulled apart eventually, not by rocks or spiny roots but by time and resentment.

"It's...a dump, Joshua. It's unfinished. Why did your father give you this mausoleum?"

"Don't be so down. Open your eyes. The very things you're criticizing are what I love about it. So, we have to fix it up. Who cares? It will be *ours* to make what we want of it. Our own little world. Our home. I can fix the floors, the kitchen, the, um...whatever this room is in here."

From where she stood, it looked like he was referring to what should've been a bathroom. She didn't dare ask him to do a test flush.

"And the ceilings too?" she added, arching an eyebrow.

"And the ceiling too," he returned, blinking as a splash of water stabbed his forehead. After rubbing the damp crease, he touched one of the walls to feel for divots or cracks in need of spackle. Some of the hallways had hideous wallpaper glued on. "The walls could use a little work, but I can manage it. I bet I can restore them back to their former beauty. All it takes is time."

Mary meandered toward the staircase, which she knew she was to assume had been wondrous once upon a time. Several spindles were missing—broken off from age, or forcefully removed? The finish had all but chipped away, faded from what was left. She refused to venture up the way Joshua so unashamedly did.

"Did you actually live here at some point?" she asked.

"When I was a boy, but I...I must've forgotten it. The mind is a funny thing. It chooses what it wants to remember."

"I can only guess why you blotted it out," she grumbled under her breath. With little more than a blink, her mind began to strip and paint these walls, to furnish these rooms, in an attempt to remind herself that not all beauty was lost.

She sought to give it life. But she couldn't finish it. She just wasn't able to finish it.

"Mary, this *mausoleum*, as you call it, was only *part* of my father's estate. He worked hard for what he earned, and he lost much of it during the recession. But this, this house was always his favorite. And he left it to me. I mean, can you believe that?"

"Joshua, forgive my skepticism here, but are we walking through the same house?"

"Of course we are." His voice echoed from above. He had already reached the top of the staircase and started across the middle hallway, which led to the other side. At the center hung a grand chandelier. In spite of the webbing and flickering light, the jewel casing still managed to sparkle.

"I just don't see it the way you do. Will this ever really feel like home? I mean, we both work hard, and we don't spend enough quality time together as it is. I just don't see how we're going to fix this place up."

He rushed down the flight of stairs, coughing up some dust after trying to take a deep breath. "Mary, you know me. You know I'm good with my hands, have been since I was a teenager. I'm an architect, for crying out loud. I know carpentry, and I know how to tile and spackle, and you're a genius with a paintbrush. Plus, don't let the cursory stuff blind you. I can figure most things out when the occasion calls for it."

"And what about all the wiring and electricity issues? Are you an expert at that as well?"

"Why do you hate this place so much?"

Mary glanced at the outdated wallpaper and the eerie, unfurnished grand foyer. What was she missing? What could Joshua see in this empty space that was so lovely? She wished for her artistic vision to kick in at any time like it had a few brief moments ago.

"I do not *hate* this place," she responded. "I'm just not sure it's us. I'm not sure it's *me*."

Joshua reached for her hands. "But I can make it anything you want it to be. Your wish is my command."

"As long as I don't wish for more wishes, right?" Mary replied, smirking.

"Precisely. I know I can make you happy here. I know you'll love it. Besides, I haven't shown you the best part."

Joshua guided her down another long hallway. There were so many rooms. At any minute, she'd be bracing herself for a crypt-kept mummy to leap out of one of the naked bookshelves and suck the life from her bones. Or maybe some reckless jewel thief would drill up through the floor in search of a safe full of diamonds. After all, a big house means a big bank account, right?

Not a chance. Mary was still waiting for her art to take off. She'd just painted a portrait of the mayor. In all honesty, she was a little ashamed at how desperate she'd become. In the past, Mary had turned down the chance to paint politicians or overtly religious images because both were topics she'd rather not get involved in—the former for societal convictions and the latter for reasons she'd never divulged to anyone, not even the man she planned to marry. The man now leading her through dimly lit, cobwebbed halls and grand banquet rooms she couldn't ever picture filling with enough legitimate house-guests. The bedrooms were located on the second and third floors, along with a number of bathrooms, great and small.

"You might be able to fix a leaky pipe, Joshua, but do you really think you can keep a place this size clean?"

"Can we do a rain check on that answer, baby?"

Mary ran her fingers through her hair, checking for webs. "That's what I thought."

"I'm only kidding. Once you sell those masterpiece paint-ings of yours and make it big, we'll just hire a maid."

It was odd how their voices echoed off the walls. They were so narrow but still capable of dragging human sound anywhere they wanted. Did these walls view them as intruders or was that just her subconscious looking for a way out?

Rain check on that answer, Mary, she told herself, slightly curious as to where her fearless fiancé would take her.

Being led somewhere with a blindfold was one of those things girls tended to fantasize about during adolescence. There was something romantic about not knowing which way to go, about listening to the sound of nothing but your footsteps and someone else's voice. But here she had no blindfold. The gentle strokes of her feet atop the tired, out-dated carpet runner weren't a peaceful sound. Instead there was Joshua's luring and the glass shelves she surmised once housed weapons too heavy for her to carry. But she was thank-ful there weren't any grizzly bear heads covering the walls.

"Almost there, my love." Joshua's sweet whisper took her from her worries, such listless distractions. Wherever was he taking her?

She lost count of her steps. She lost count of how many times she let slip an anxious breath. She ignored the fact that they had to wander nearly the entire lower half of the mansion to find the location her fiancé was looking for.

Finally, they arrived.

Mary paused when she saw how awestruck Joshua's face was. How perfectly still each muscle in his jaw sat or the manner in which he took his next breath.

He fumbled around the dank-smelling room, more like an afterthought garage. It resembled a metal cage.

When the outside lampposts flashed, her eyes followed the light.

"Isn't it unlike anything you've ever seen?" Joshua asked before she had the chance to speak.

Even when the opportunity presented itself, she was at a loss for words. Her eyes were   xed on the circular garden outside. By far, the most lovely and peaceful scene of the entire property.

"But how can this be?" she asked. "Everything about this place is so dilapidated, ruined. But this little garden...."

"Little?" Joshua said, turning on the remainder of the outside fixtures. It looked like Christmas, the grand, artificial glow warring against the night. Other sections of the enormous structure surrounded the garden, which sat at the center of everything.

After he unlocked the rickety door, Joshua let her walk the brick-laid path his father completed many years before. "What's the first word that comes to your mind?

"Breathtaking," Mary responded without hesitation.

"I thought you'd like it. My father believed that as long as the garden remained intact, everything else would fall into place."

"But it didn't, Joshua," she argued, still unsure how it was that so much brilliance could be confined to such forgettable mansion walls. "His home became ugly."

"Time tests all things. But I think it was always meant to be mine." He grinned. "Ours. I can restore it."

He hadn't made an oath to do so, but oaths weren't necessary; Mary knew by Joshua's tone that he meant what he said. She walked inside the garden. She was home. Here and in her youth. She was fourteen and tomorrow. Flowers of every variety and shape and color reached up out of the dirt like resurrected, painted souls. The fireflies had returned, flickering all around her. She looked back at her lover for a moment then focused once more on the jewel of this mausoleum.

"Of all the greenhouses and meadows I've seen, Joshua, nothing, nothing at all compares." Was it normal for her to feel like she might cry? Was she supposed to start choking up from only a glimpse? But no, she had *touched* the flowers. She had smelled them. She had placed her hands into the dirt, into the earth to feel nature's art for herself. She knew it was real. Her senses, her eyes, her everything confirmed it.

This was a new memory. And this one tasted like honey.

After Mary walked through the garden, exploring it from every angle, Joshua called her and asked if she was ready to see the remainder of the house. Still taken aback at the sheer size of the house, Mary nodded. Joshua had already made his rounds once through the many corridors and entrances. Getting familiar with a place might make it feel more like home, he suggested to her. But she didn't much care about what surrounded the garden that seemed to defy all pattern and prediction. It didn't fit with everything else. *Not yet*, she could almost hear Joshua echoing in her eardrum.

A deep sigh and a long breath permitted her leave followed by one last blink to capture the perfect image.

"I'm ready," she said with an enchanted smile.

It didn't take long to walk through the rest of the mansion. The fact that she kept a steady pace ahead of her fiancé didn't at all add to the romance of seeing the place for the first time, but she felt how she felt, and he couldn't begrudge her for that, could he? She was an artist, so to see something beyond the ugly and malnourished should've been effortless. She would try. She swore to herself she would try.

The garden still had her mind tightly in its grasp. Its thin, winding passages and overhanging branches dripping with splashes of life. Blink upon blink she returned there, while Joshua carried on about how much torque it must've taken his great-grandfather to put this building together. And here it was, still standing. She couldn't help but tune in to the important parts.

Her nostrils finally took note of the smell. It wasn't a horrible smell, necessarily. It was a kind of smell like she'd just walked into Grandma's house and wasn't sure if the smell made her comfortable or if she'd get used to it eventually. She'd read somewhere that everything was eventual. How true that was. After some flaring, and several deep breaths through her nostrils, she settled herself and got used to the smell. The *eventual* came pretty quickly this time.

It was hard to believe that it had taken them less than thirty minutes to walk through the mansion, but Mary was happy. After all, she'd ventured out past the dock and into strange waters. That was unlike her. A sense of bravery flooded in. Sitting at home in sweats and watching painful television wouldn't have been nearly as invigorating as seeing the garden in full bloom, and still at the starting line of spring. She could only imagine how brilliant the flowers might look in the coming season.

"When can we start fixing it up?" she asked, like an eager child.

"I thought you didn't like the place. It was dark and unwelcoming, wasn't it?"

"Yes," she said with a slight nod, the smile still hanging on. "But that garden, Joshua, there was something about it that just...I can't explain it."

"Good grief, that's all it took? If I knew it would make that much of an impression, I would've started the tour from the back." Joshua shut the front door and fidgeted with the lock until he was sure it was secure. Mary stood on the porch, gazing out over what would someday be hers.

"Of course I left the light on in the foyer," Joshua said sarcastically, searching for the key. With a mini flashlight pinched between his teeth, he struggled to find it.

Mary was taken from the porch for a moment. Her eyes drifted to the willow tree planted on the front lawn. Its roots stretched across the dirt-and-pebble driveway and a number of other spots around its formidable trunk. At first, Mary squinted to see what was carved at the center. She walked down the porch steps to get a clearer look. Joshua didn't notice. He was busy jangling his keys and trying to break in out of frustration because the lock now refused to budge.

As she edged closer, the carving in the willow tree became clearer. It was a solitary word no one would raise a question about. A forgettable something, really. Nothing elaborate or poetic. Just simple, scratched into the bark. It read, *Once.*

Who put it here? she wondered.

Just then, Mary glimpsed a shadow from the road that led to their future driveway, which she could see herself pressuring Joshua to get paved as soon as humanly possible. The shadow captured her glance when she touched the tree, felt the cut-up pieces that comprised the fragile, infant word. She swore she saw a face too with the shadow. It was a man with a soft complexion and a beard. A black hat kept his long hair neat and tucked. He had on a lengthy coat as well, and his teeth appeared yellow, glistening in the moonlight as he smiled at her from the road.

But then he was gone. Suddenly, a fog drifted in from the woods, and the chill forced her to blink. And shudder a little. She turned on the spot and saw Joshua coming closer.

She reached for his arm.

"What's got you all jumpy?" he asked.

"It's awful dark out here."

"Yeah. Looks like we'll have to get used to that," Joshua said. "Hmm, did you notice our voices echo out here too?" Without awaiting a response, he repeated, "Echo!"

"Stop it," she demanded.

"Why?"

"Because you never know who could be out this time of night."

Tell him, Mary. Tell him what you saw. Tell him you saw

a man, well, what looked like a man, with long hair and a beard and a black hat and....

That is what you saw, isn't it?

"I got cold all of a sudden, Joshua. I want to head back now."

"Okay," he said, embracing her. "Let's get you warm." He unlocked the car with the keyless entry device.

Mary immediately went for the passenger door and sank into her seat, fastening her belt as tight as it would go. Joshua walked slowly, however, intensifying the tension inside her.

Just tell him what you saw.

Mary shut her eyes and pictured the garden. Maybe her mind had invented the man in black. Her mind had invented things and ideas before, so it wasn't all that strange, was it? An imagination could be a dangerous thing, a very dangerous thing, the years had taught her.

Joshua opened the driver's side door and slipped into his seat. He started the car and backed out. Mary looked out the window as a branch scraped the front hood. She couldn't help but feel saddened by the carving there in the heart of the willow tree. In a matter of seconds, they were backing out of the driveway, leaving the property of the mansion, and heading back to the city.

Summer

1

THERE WAS CHANGE AGAIN IN the air. The June sunlight invaded her apartment, and the heat started to get to her.
At least, Mary blamed her anxiety on the heat, an appropriate
scapegoat.

She was glad to admit she sensed something a little more
alive in herself lately. Her mind often returned to the garden
and the beauty it held. It wasn't that her doubts about the
mansion itself had evaporated, because they hadn't fully. But
with these winds of change came confidence and ambition.
She was closer to accepting the future, even if part of her—
most of her—feared it.

Maybe Joshua's constant imagination about what the
mansion *could be* kept her mind running in circles.

A collection of cardboard boxes lined the walls of her
cramped bedroom. The beaten, pulled-open worlds
seemed to act as mirrors, reflections of the way she
had been dealing with it all up until today. Week upon
week she had been second-guessing the decision to move
the wedding up a few months so they could begin working
on the mansion together and be rid of the expenses of renting

separate apartments. She'd already been convinced that calling the property anything other than a mansion was a gross understatement. But the open boxes, which she was prepared to fill with all of the important things inside this room—in her life—still lay bar-ren. Unaccomplished. Unfulfilled.

Mary massaged her temples, wondering what should go into the boxes first and which items belonged in which box. Did she have to categorize them with black marker before filling them or after filling them? Was it appropriate yet to label boxes *Mary's Stuff* and some *Joshua's Stuff*? After all, some of his college t-shirts had found their way into her dressers, and several of his movies had wandered into her collection during their brief engagement. But he hadn't forgotten any of these things, she was certain. He'd left them behind on purpose so that one day he could come back for them, with her here to greet him as his bride.

He was that shameless romantic most girls read about in what she liked to call "fever novels" because all of her pathetic friends—both of them—fell victim to the simplistic writing and predictable plots offered by the long-winded sagas. She'd never be a victim of the typical, boring lullabies, even if she truly did adore the *idea* of love.

Mary whispered Joshua's name just to gain focus. For some strange reason, reminding her heart of him ushered in a bit of peace. If he were here, he'd know what to do. He'd know how to arrange the items into the boxes; he'd categorize everything the proper way; he might even misplace certain things as his way of checking to see if she were actually present or if she'd mentally checked out because moving in together as husband and wife might allow for certain unintentional complications to creep into the relationship.

"It's gonna be all right. Stop freaking out. There is no reason to doubt, not anymore. I love you." Joshua murmured these serene comments to her just then. Sure, the syllables escaped from *her* lips, but it was exactly what he would've said.

If she could, she would paint something. But not before tucking her collections and the stuff she hardly used but still believed she wanted into the boxes neatly so they'd be ready to transport to her new home.

She started with the picture of Little Sis and herself. It had been taken at the beginning of her sophomore year of high school, after the move. Mary was not ready then to embrace a new world of students, teachers, and troublemakers who'd spout off vicious nicknames she'd eventually identify with come junior year. It was the students' way of leaving their mark on her, she imagined, their way of living forever inside her. She eventually painted some of the kids too, as creatures doing dreadful things. Ugly, scorned images. In fact, sophomore year ushered in the darkest memory, when one of the malicious creatures wounded her.

The creature, more adequately described as a senior boy,

had gotten too rough in one of the locker rooms. It was a mistake being there at night. She shouldn't have been so naïve to think he actually had feelings for her after a semester's worth of ridicule. Groping her chest came first. He rubbed her crudely, like a greedy kid in a candy store, snickering the whole time and saying he couldn't find her breasts beneath the fabric. Harder and harder he squeezed her underdeveloped chest, until her skin felt raw. After he obtained satisfaction, he dropped his mouth from hers and started to pull at her chilled neck with his teeth. They were like scissors.

She didn't show Mom or Dad the bruises. She didn't tell a soul. Not with words anyway. But she painted it. And it was a sad painting. It was a splattered, morbid mess that told the story clearly, that embodied every bit of unhappiness and displeasure she had endured. What she had been forced to live with.

The emotions were taken somewhere far away, she hoped. Farther away than the distance of time she now existed from her beloved sister. The space this photograph made real again. "Thanks, Sis," she said sarcastically, "for bringing the memory back."

She was wrong to blame Jamie, and she knew it.

Over the years, Mary imagined the painting put up in some secret room where no children were allowed to play. Where no love was permitted. It was a dark place, the way this one was starting to feel now that she'd called such a memory out of her nightmares again. Now that the photograph of her sister started to bend in her grip, the frame ready to snap. She imagined a plume of smoke stretching across the painting she had created out of the tormented chambers of her heart. She named the painting "Past" and didn't bother filling in any details for the enchanted buyer. The man who purchased it claimed the piece possessed such life, such tenacity and brilliance and raw emotion. *Like the fever novels*, she mused when he'd given her the compliment, along with a two thousand-dollar check.

Of course, *he* didn't know that the picture had been the offspring of one of the worst nights in her life, birthed in immeasurable pain. How could memories do this? How could they get away with causing so much heartache? Where were the judges who let this atrocity occur? Where were the school kids? Where were the angels and saints?

Where was Joshua?

Her phone vibrated in her pocket. She wasn't wearing much: some ripped jeans, a loose tank, no socks. She pinned up her hair like a prisoner, locks pulled back from misting eyes. Mary didn't notice that the picture's glass had cut her hand until she decided to answer the call.

"Sweetheart, it's me. How are you? You okay?" She could tell that he knew. He knew before she even said a word that something was not right.

"I was just thinking," she replied, sniffling.

"Are you crying? What happened?"

"Just thinking. I got distracted, cut my hand a little on an old picture."

"The picture of you and Jamie?"

"Yeah. How'd you know?"

"Mary, it's the only photograph in your bedroom. You said you were packing up the stuff in there today."

"Right. Look, when, when are you coming over tonight? I miss you."

"Is it all right if I like being missed?" He must've been hoping that little comment would make her smile, but it didn't.

"I suppose. Takeout? Seven?" she asked.

"Yeah," he said. "And don't stress too much. It's a beautiful day. I think it'd be a good idea for you to get out for awhile. Enjoy the sunshine. It's been raining far too much lately. Seems the weather guy finally got something right. Get out for bit to get some fresh air. It'll relieve any stress."

"Yeah, you're probably right."

"I love you, you know."

"Yeah," she weakly said. The blood had dripped a little onto the carpet. She already lamented the scrubbing that would be required to get the red stain out so her landlady didn't charge her upon vacating the apartment. The ornery old crow was the kind who didn't miss a thing.

"I can't believe we're getting married in less than two months."

"Yeah, it seemed so far before, but it really came quick."

Was it hitting her for the first time? Really hitting her? Mary decided to sit down on the bed. "You still sure you wanna marry a neurotic artist with issues?"

"You still sure you wanna marry a workaholic who claims he can fix up a broken-down mansion?" he commented back.

"Not sure," she said, half-smiling. "Maybe I should have my people call your people at the office and tell them the whole thing is off."

She was glad he embraced her comment with a chuckle. She wasn't sure what she'd do if he didn't laugh to set her mind at ease. But deep down, it wasn't a joke at all.

2

JOSHUA HUNG UP THE PHONE and stared at his computer screen for a moment. Suddenly the design of a new skyscraper didn't seem that important. Mary's doubts were getting harder to battle, which was the reason he had extended his hours and had become selective at when they saw each other. It wasn't that he didn't want to be with her; it was that every time he got close, hearing the quiver in her voice or seeing the slant in her eye when she murmured that she loved him, intensified the sting.

As a boy, he'd envisioned his life a little differently. Making it through high school without getting into trouble. Going to college to be one of the world's most esteemed architects. Graduating with a fiancée who would love him as much as he'd love her. But these snapshots never told the whole story, only glimpsed it in oddly arranged photographs. They never let him in on the fact that, though these things would come, they'd come in their own time. He'd gone to school—several schools, actually—but more in search of the right woman than the right degree program. Why? Why did it matter so much with whom he spent his life? Why did it become such a burden?

"Because we're made to love," his father had told him when he was young. "We are made to love." Five words he still couldn't fathom completely. It was in him to be this way, to throw his heart and soul into a person, even if that person didn't know what to do with it. It wasn't some kind of calculation; it was part of who he was. Transfer student looking for love. His roommates often snickered at his lofty ideals, at his always believing that his true romance could be found.

Joshua graduated. But the soulmate he had longed for since he could remember wasn't there to see him get his diploma, to see that he could finish something and finish it strong.

Contemplative, Joshua leaned back in his chair and loosened his tie. Through the glass doors of his office, he saw his best friend, Matthew. The one who had invited him to the art gallery downtown one night after work. The one who introduced him to the love of his life.

"Better late than never, right?" Matthew whispered into his ear when they both noticed Mary's slender figure from across the room. Her art was breathtaking, but it was more than her talent which attracted him to her, he knew. She was showing off one of her pieces from the collection to an elderly couple when he invented a reason to interrupt and ask her to dinner.

Matthew had always been a good friend. Joshua was grateful

to have him as one of the few people from college with whom he remained in contact. Always the wingman. The decision to hire him as an executive had been an easy one to make.

"Better late than never," Joshua said with a sigh. Perhaps that was the lens through which he had to view Mary. Several weeks came and went before she decided to finally open up to him for real. She agreed to his dinner date, but only because of his persistence that night and because her eyes couldn't find a justifiable reason to escape his. She agreed to more dates because he continually found excuses to run into her on his walks home from the firm. The fact that her gallery sat just a few blocks away compelled him to drop by whenever possible. But even when he proposed, she hesitated. Why was there always this hesitation?

"Women are complicated creatures, man," Matthew had said during a game of pool after Joshua had been seeing Mary for some time, but it wasn't anything he didn't already know. He didn't want average, boring love. He craved intellect and a challenge.

No, Mary's more than just some challenge. Joshua scratched the corner of his mouth, wishing he'd never even thought that low of her. He was so sure of his love, sure that maybe she had started out as a beautiful challenge, but that she was now a lover he could not imagine being without.

A lover who just needed time to come around. Folding his arms, he prayed it was true.

3

THE DESIGNER REMOVED MARY'S VEIL and asked her what she thought of the wedding dress.

"It's..." *Just finish the sentence.* Why couldn't she just finish the sentence? The dress was captivating, magical, everything she'd dreamed of and more. But the words were stuck behind her unflinching tongue.

The material made her waist appear more slender than she expected. She liked that about the gown. She had always been self-conscious when it came to her arms too, but even they looked seductive once slipped inside comfortable lace sleeves. This was a work of art, uniquely designed. The sleeves complemented the dress's feathered bottom with grace. Thin straps held the top section of the dress and wrapped around the back of Mary's neck. Normally, that spot was where much of the tension in her spine dwelled, but today she didn't feel a thing.

Then tell the woman it looks like a dream, or have they not invented a pill for that yet?

"Well?" the designer asked again. "What do you think?"

What did she think? She wasn't supposed to come here alone. The afternoon was intended to be a chance for her and Jamie to bond. They hadn't hung out in weeks. But Little Sis canceled on her due to "husband" trouble, whatever that meant. It was curious that Jamie had managed to walk the aisle before Mary had even thought about it. But where was she now? At home, most likely rummaging through a myriad of bills in a crowded house with a teething two-year-old.

Is that what I have to look forward to?

She cared so deeply for Joshua. A love is what she'd call it, but was it that, really? Was someone like her even capable of pure love?

"It's wonderful," Mary finally said, blinking at her reflection.

"Does everything fit all right?" the designer asked, tape measure pinched between her jaws as she stood tautly across the room in order to get a more accurate view.

"It fits fine," Mary said. She thought about her sister. She thought about the possible future she might be pressured to accept. Or worse, she thought about the end. Half of marriages succeeded and half didn't make it to see their kids through high school. Pathetic how simply love could be boiled down to a statistic. A lifeline in some stupid game show no one even watched anymore.

"I really do love this dress," she admitted, this time slightly more sure.

The designer now had the relief she had been looking for.

"I can just picture it, the wedding of the year," the woman said. "And with the right earrings and necklace, this dress will truly take his breath away."

"I'm sure it will," Mary replied, gently stroking her waist and tilting her head as she gazed into her reflection at the girl who had become a high school student, a college dropout, an artist, and a wife in a blink. It was never an age thing; it was a mind thing. For all her sister's flaws, Jamie knew how to do one thing right: She knew how to make a choice.

"I was married once," the designer said after Mary had changed out of the dress. "I once was *in love*. Treasure it, my dear. I lost the love of my life, and I can tell you truly to love whatcha got. Treasure it because that's all life is about. That's the real stuff."

Mary caught her reflection one last time. She wouldn't end up a widow like this broken artist. That wasn't her. If she were to be a word, any word at all, she prayed it was *forever*.

And then she pictured the mysterious man with a black hat standing in the middle of the road just glaring at her. She could still make out his piercing eyes.

A chill ran down her spine as Mary made a reservation to pick up the dress a few days before the wedding. She breathed a long, deep sigh. She was weary of all her doubts. She was tired of fighting them back. If they could just die, she might have peace.

Mary replaced the jumble in her head with thoughts of the

wedding. When she stepped out of the store and into the warm sun, city traffic, and the confusion of every day, she smiled a full but still conflicted smile.

What if the widow was right, and life could be consumed by love? Perhaps it had the power to rapture her entire body.

The wedding was so close now. She hoped Joshua would think her as magical as she wanted to see herself. She hoped his love might endure beyond the worn-out statistics.

Mary waited until the traffic signs assured her it was safe to cross to the other side. Her apartment waited for her, no more than a few blocks down. With the breeze gently tossing her hair back, she no longer dreaded returning home to finish collecting her things. Like that wretched painting she'd packed away a few weeks earlier, her apartment was the past, and Joshua's mansion had to be the future she needed more than she knew.

The air would be freer now. Her heart would become quiet.

Mary chewed her bottom lip. Maybe she didn't have to go back to her place just yet. Maybe she'd surprise Joshua with a late lunch instead.

9

AUGUST SUNSETS WERE BREATHTAKING. The trees appeared graceful as they prepared for the fall season, when their leaves would change colors again and slip away. The scattered street lights occasionally pierced the glass. Mary pondered the wedding ceremony, now just hours behind her. It was an admittedly brief service and an even briefer reception. There was no limousine to carry them to the airport for a European getaway. She and Joshua had opted out of an extravagant honeymoon and instead decided to begin working on the mansion.

"It's romantic if you think about it," she told Jamie over a glass of wine at the reception, to which Jamie just rolled her eyes.

Mary's Pathfinder was a logical choice for the Sunday drive. She had come to terms with the uprooting of her intense life in the city and moving to the tranquil and obscure routes this woodsy town offered. Her full trunk and cab bothered Joshua a great deal more than they did her. Mary had determined to fit all the necessities from her bedroom, including her painting supplies and canvases, into the SUV. "That's what these trucks are made for, isn't it?" she remarked upon departing the apartment. Joshua's lethargic shrug insinuated there would be slight discomfort, but she just assumed he was overreacting.

With each blink, Mary relived their vows, the unusual squint the priest gave them when she swung her arms around Joshua's sweet-smelling neck and employed tongue during their first kiss as a married couple. The small audience, consisting of a few college acquaintances and the family members who could make it, didn't mind the spectacle. In fact, several cheered. It was like being transported back to a high school pep rally in which she was the star. Felt kinda nice. Even if making out on the altar might have been a little unorthodox, it was so worth it.

It had been an energetic, nearly perfect day, and much to her surprise, the wedding had gone off with only a few hiccups, one being the awkward walk toward the altar arm-locked to her brother-in-law. Little Sis insisted it be him who filled in for Dad. And ever since they were kids, Jamie got her way if she pushed hard enough. Seeing as how every wedding was secretly an opportunity for sisters to live vicariously, Mary caved. It was the least she could do following the years of support she'd had since Mom and Dad's deaths.

Mary rounded the next corner slightly faster than the speed limit. She noticed Joshua's uneasiness immediately when he pretended to vomit into the new Chanel purse she'd received as a wedding gift from an aunt she hadn't spoken to in years but somehow claimed to have gotten an invitation. "My driving is *not* that bad, mister," she said, the SUV falling back in line with the white paint on the road.

Joshua rolled his eyes. "Can I still vomit in the purse?"

"No, you cannot. Now, put it down and no one gets hurt."

"All right. I still can't believe your aunt dropped several hundred bucks on this thing."

"It's high-class art, honey. Some people just don't get it. Although, I am a little curious how she got invited in the first place."

"It was probably Jamie," he replied, putting the purse near his feet. "Your sister loves to talk and start drama. I'll bet she imagined inviting your aunt might get you worked up."

"I don't even think my aunt remembers why we fought in the first place. Besides, it was my wedding day, and I think we kept things amicable. You know, that old lady can dance."

"Tell me about it."

She took a deep breath. "I can't believe we did it. I mean, we're married," Mary said, making sure to take the next turn with more grace. "Like, really married."

"The wedding was something, wasn't it, sweetheart?"

She nodded.

"You don't think the guests were offended by our cutting it short, do you? Think it was rude?"

Mary shrugged.

"She pleads the fifth, huh? Always so opinionated, and all of a sudden she's got nothing to say."

"Look, I had a great time. Isn't that what matters...*husband?*" The term of endearment still felt strange rolling off her lips, but she liked it. "Besides, I think the guests had fun."

"Yeah, my cousin wouldn't stop hitting on your sister, even though I told him last night she was off the market."

"I believe 'somebody else's ball and chain' was the term you so eloquently used."

He looked stunned.

"Yeah," Mary said, "your cousin gets awfully chatty after a few drinks."

"Perhaps I need to keep my conversations a little more top secret," Joshua said, fidgeting with the sunroof that just wouldn't close.

Mary slapped his knee twice.

"I mean, sorry?"

"Joshua," she said with a sigh. "You don't really think that, do you?"

"Think what?"

"That I'm your ball and chain?"

"Of course not. That's just something guys say to other guys. But let's be fair, your sister's a little...well, she's your sister. Look, it was nothing more than a joke, really. You, my love, are so much more than that."

"Oh?" she answered coyly when he kissed her cheek.

"You're my...cellmate for life."

"For the record, that isn't funny."

"No, it's a good thing. I swear," he said, planting another kiss on her rosy cheek. "You make me feel all bubbly and tingly inside." He couldn't keep a straight face while trying to formulate a suitable comeback.

"I guess I'll take it."

"You know I'm just messing with you, right? About Jamie? I don't hate her. She's pretty cool. Well, tolerable...in a slightly neurotic, control-freak kinda way."

"Hey, I can be neurotic too."

"Oh, you have a valid point. Well, I guess I love you anyway."

"Gee...how sweet."

Joshua leaned over and gently stroked her neck, her lips. Then his eyes fell to the dress and back up again.

"Why are you staring at me like that?" she asked.

"Like what?"

"Like you're seeing me for the first time.

"Well, Mrs. Clay, I do believe I am seeing you for the first time, as my wife."

"I like it when you call me that."

"My bride."

Her cheeks flushed a deeper shade of red

"My beautiful...gorgeous...ball and chain."

She playfully grunted.

"Still hasn't grown on you yet, has it?" Joshua replied with arched eyebrows. "Noted."

"I love you, you know," Mary said at length. "I think I really love you."

"Well, I'm glad that after three years of dating, an engagement, and ultimately our wedding vows, this epiphany has finally hit you. I was starting to worry."

"Cut it out, you goofball. I mean it." Her shoulders climbed to her neck as she bit her lower lip. "I love you, Joshua."

"I love you too, Mary. My beautiful bride."

She relived Joshua's hands slowly lifting up her veil. He gazed into her eyes, and he resolved the war behind them with one touch. The late summer morning held their faces in calm. She could see what looked like sparrows floating effortlessly in the air. It should've been humid, uncomfortable in that dress, in his hands, but it wasn't. His boyish grin, his slick, combed-through hair, those disarming eyes, had power.

As Joshua read his vows, her heart began to warm within her chest. Every breath a stutter. A joy. She again looked out on the small crowd of people who had watched her wander down the aisle toward the altar during the softest of songs. Thankfully, she didn't trip, not like her sister. She was his bride now. She had a new song, like the sparrows tweeting above them in the close-by trees while the priest ended their ceremony by asking Joshua to kiss her.

Why was there ever any doubt or fear? Joshua's mouth

had penned a brilliant story across her lips when he touched them for the first time as her husband. Passion and unbridled faith consumed each breath. Among the things she tasted were his dreams, his sweet cologne, and the flowers from the surrounding meadow. *Like my garden.*

What she smelled now, however, was some of the food the caterers had allowed them to package and take along with what was left of their wedding cake. While never being a fan of fondant cakes, Mary knew this one tasted richer. She and Joshua would spend the upcoming week working on the mansion during the day, polishing off the remainder of the food at dusk, and wrapped in each other's arms at night.

Upon their arrival, Mary parked the Pathfinder and waited for Joshua to come around to the driver's side and indulge her teenage fantasy of being lifted out of the carriage by someone strong and handsome.

"How romantic of you," Mary said when he took her by the arm and clumsily lifted her over his shoulder.

"Is this how you do it?" he asked.

"Not in the slightest, husband."

"Oh, look at that. The word isn't on her lips twenty-four hours before she's using it all negatively."

"Well, if you would carry me like a lady, then I would gladly use your title more romantically."

Joshua chuckled. He placed her down and picked her back up again properly but not before planting one on her mouth.

"You know you love my sense of humor."

"I suppose it is rather cute," she said, licking her lips to savor his taste.

"Shall we enter our humble abode now, m'lady?"

"Certainly, my handsome prince." As Joshua carried her across the lawn, she couldn't help but glance for a moment at the sad willow tree. It sought to rob her of this moment of happiness. She imagined it as some other lost girl, a child who once glimpsed hope but was now riddled with sorrow and age and the realities of the world, only capable of expelling new miseries to those who still clung to the frailties of life. Mary tucked her head into Joshua's firm chest. Once at the porch, she reached into his pocket and searched for the right key.

"I think I found the one," she said, staring into his eyes. She placed the key in the handle and turned it until the door opened.

"Now, why is it whenever I try to do that, the door fights me?"

"Because, my dear, this lock cannot resist my charms."

He let her down upon entering the mansion's front door. It was barely dusk, and the light would continue to trickle in for the next hour or so. Mary danced with joy for the first time in the foyer she had once despised. Suddenly, it didn't matter that the mansion remained an unfinished painting. She knew this place could be home.

"You look like magic," Joshua said, beaming as he reached for her hand for their second first dance.

Fall

1

BY THE END OF SEPTEMBER, dawn resembled dark poetry. A spellbound earth sat behind the hills and clouds and dim but rising light. It was made new by irregular colors. The trees on the south end of the mansion flexed rebelliously out of the black dirt womb and created skinny branches. The shades of leaves faded. Mary imagined mutinous veins charging up the bark of its tree—the very same wires that showed the lifeline of every leaf that would soon slip off to die—as a nearly invisible force that plagued the world. The world was so unbalanced. When would she be able to explain the mystery of death? The mystery of change? Or perhaps no clean answer existed for why things were lost. Perhaps only the fallow grounds of the earth displayed the questions with similar unfinished lines.

Mary blinked and realized the sunrise had already come, and she had missed its final movement. She turned her gaze from the strange reality of nature to her still canvas—a pale, man-made thing desperate to come alive again with a fresh soul. Her painting had no beginning and no end. Where was her inspiration?

Mary touched her stomach. Life had been replaced by hate. "The hope I dreamed is gone from me," she said with tears crawling from her eyes. Her left hand was still on her belly, waiting for there to be a spike of pain or a stir. Nothing. The paintbrush in her right hand snapped in half. *It was made to be broken*, she thought.

The light reaching down from a sky with no conviction seemed like a curse. There was no common ground in her, she knew that now more than ever. Maybe there had never been. She was purgatory, if such a wretched place could be conceived while wives were left empty.

The sounds of her husband hammering in the hallway less than fifty feet away encompassed her. Every time he swung against that drywall, she felt her brain brush up against her skull, wondering if ever he'd hit it hard enough to render her unconscious.

The center of her quivered at the thought of being reunited with him. He didn't deserve to have her. Nor did the sky, with all of its apathy and neglect. Stuck in this spot. Stuck in this house. Stuck in this body with no life. Her roots had been planted deep, with no true comprehension that these grounds would seek to contain her for eternities no dream could compose.

Bang! Crash! Bang! Movement with no purpose. What was the point of fixing this place? Jamie had called just an hour earlier, and she could hear her nephew's laugh in the background. An adolescent's laugh never sounded so sublime.

Morning gone. Afternoon replaced by night. Mary was stuck in the sunrise that refused to show its face again. The summers she swore she would mourn time after time.

Beside the glass of water that now possessed a strange, murky layer on its surface, lay an open orange bottle. Joshua could hammer until midnight if he wanted, but that wouldn't change a thing. *We all have our ways, don't we?*

Empty. Like the canvas. It would remain that way.

2

MARY CHEWED THE END OF her paint brush, not even bothering to notice that a drop of golden paint had dripped onto her night gown. The wooden stand her canvas sat on appeared shaky and unsure of itself. The wide-open lattice doors behind her, which Joshua had recently finished to complete their bedroom, swayed. Her husband lay asleep in bed. The propped-open doors allowed her free passing onto the outside deck, where she'd set up, though it was becoming more of a habit than anything.

The southern landscape seemed beautiful, more beautiful than she felt. Envy festered inside her when she saw the lush, green grass carpeting the grounds, overlooked by massive trees she wished to call by name. Her husband had landscaped the property so beautifully. It was strange to consider that another October was nearly complete.

The wind, much like her body, felt old.

She sat with her legs crossed under her on the stool that, on most days, she thought uncomfortable. It didn't seem to antagonize her today, though. Not like the still unfinished art in front of her. It was startling how far she'd come with it. But it seemed an impenetrable wall had been erected. She couldn't trespass, no matter how hard she tried. Looking upon the thing now was like staring into a mirror only to see something frightening.

"I missed the sunrise again." Maybe it was deliberate, maybe not.

"The sun will come up again tomorrow, baby," Joshua mumbled. He did that sometimes in his half-way sleep, rolling over to say something that was intended to calm her soul. It only frustrated her.

Mary leaned back on her stool to see if she might catch a glimpse of Joshua turning in his sleep, or if he was awake. Neither was true, she discovered. He was the sunrise she missed so strongly, perhaps, and she was the cloud that, in time, might eclipse him.

"You mustn't think that way, Mary. He loves you." Her thoughts had grown loud enough that sometimes they came out of her. While she helped him tile the bathroom floor a few nights back, she had felt the wandering notions, a few unsteady questions that wanted answers.

Is he the one? Is he all *there is? Is* this numbness *all that is left?*

The mansion still had much work to be done. Joshua often fell asleep on the floors beside a metal paddle of spackle or hands covered in glue from the wallpaper he'd spent hours peeling. Mary had made sure to capture snapshots of them restoring the mansion when she felt in control of her emotions, though such occasions were rare. She knew that she and Joshua still had to replace the light fixtures, re-carpet many of the rooms, finish painting the walls and handle the many electrical issues. Plus several furnaces were barely functional. The dream was overwhelming.

But whenever thoughts came upon her like this, in synchronized fashion, she came to realize how trivial it all seemed compared to the hole in her womb. As a young girl, she had wished to never have children, especially considering an adolescent's potential for screwing up. The boy who groped her body in that defiled high school locker room was somebody's child, wasn't he? But the reality of that wish did not fully consume her until she discovered that she had lost her own hope, her own child, and was told by the apathetic professionals that chances were slim she'd ever be able to conceive again.

The situation turned Joshua cold toward her. It made her colder toward him, even though she believed he didn't mean for his silence to stricken her like it did. They slept together, but they hadn't shared a passionate night in so long. She had already begun to forget what romance was made of, because it wasn't this.

Mary's legs had lost circulation from sitting too long on the stool. Unfolding her knees, she let her feet touch the chilled marble floor again. Joshua had made their bedroom like a palace. She blushed whenever she walked by the fireplace with a stunning mantelpiece upon which sat her favorite of their wedding photographs. It was a simple shot, black and white, with her laughing at a joke of his and him smirking because he knew he'd gotten her to break character in the pose. She loved it.

Joshua woke when she turned on the television. It hung on the wall beside one of her more creative pieces. She grimaced passing by it while a news anchor brought them the latest story. Mary hated watching the news, especially first thing in the morning, but Joshua liked it to play in the background.

"It's my world," he'd always say. "I like to know what's going on in my world." And right after that came the usual, "It's your world too, honey."

To which she replied, "Not by choice."

Was it wrong of her to become hostile when she didn't feel creative? When she existed in such a state of distraction? She'd visited an art gallery once in Newport, and the artist boldly confessed his need for failure. "It shows me that while at my worst, I am capable of finding my best," he'd said after showing a piece that took him nearly two years to complete. Something had begun in chaos but ended in beauty. There was something magical about that, even poetic.

But the creative juices seemed drained from her lately. "Simply complicated, that's what I am," she murmured, heading into the bathroom suite to brush her teeth. Joshua was so focused on his world that he missed her self-indulgent sarcasm. Mary slammed the bathroom door and locked herself inside.

3

SHE DIDN'T SPEAK TO JOSHUA unless she had to. Time passed so fast she could miss weeks with a blink. The mansion presented her with the luxury of seclusion when she wanted it. But then again, she didn't, really. She wanted to be alone, but she didn't want to *feel* lonely. And that's what she was.

Mary didn't paint anymore. There was no art that she could see. Her mind fled to better times, to summer nights in bed with Joshua. She hated this separation, but she didn't know how to fix it. She couldn't fix the way she felt, the way she thought. She couldn't bridge that divide no matter how many tears she parted with. When they worked on the mansion they were side by side but not together. She executed every sentence with abrupt precision. And he often asked what was the matter, but she never divulged the reasons for her discomfort.

Once he told her that he was willing to fight, scream if he had to, if it meant they could really talk.

"No," Mary said with defiance.

Convincing herself it was the unborn baby that had her mind all confused seemed normal and logical. But that was an even bigger lie than the ring on her finger. In fact, the more she pondered it, the more she believed *she* was the lie, and the fact that she purposely wore garments several sizes too big so Joshua would find little pleasure in her appearance swelled her with shame. But that shame wasn't powerful enough to make her change. She had a right to feel how she felt. No one should judge her for that.

Mary was in the garden when Joshua decided to come and speak with her. "What's the matter, Mary?"

She gave him silence. Payment for the silence he'd first given her.

"What happened to us?"

Mary touched new, blooming flowers with her fingertips and caught the tears before they fell. It was a miracle they were still alive. "I think I need to be alone today. I think I just need to be alone." She wanted him to stay but not to speak, not to judge her.

He touched her shoulder, leaving behind a mark. His hands were stained with polyurethane, the coating he put on some of the floors in the mansion that made parts of the home smell pungent and bitter.

"Look at me. This has to stop sometime. I hate what has become of us. You're my wife! I love you. There's nothing we can't face together. Please just talk to me."

She pulled away.

"It's okay. It wasn't your fault."

"You think that's what this is about? That's it, huh? Is that all you ever think about? How I lost your child?"

"No. I know that's what you have come to believe, but it isn't the truth."

"You're a liar."

Joshua stared into her. "Please. You don't have to do this. Talk to me. You woke up angry again today, locked yourself in the bathroom for hours. You do it so often I don't even bother you anymore. My goodness, have you even eaten anything?"

She folded her arms and looked away.

"Baby, we don't talk anymore, and you're so distant. I'm here. I want to be close to you."

She swallowed hard. "I don't feel right anymore, Joshua. I've tried for so long, but I'm not right. I know I'm not right." She stroked her belly and swore there was a thick pool of blood staining her hands. "I'm empty, but I'm full of...of... rage. Bitterness." She looked down then looked up again. "Hate. You can't understand."

"You don't ever let me try!"

She shoved him in the chest. "You could never understand. I have this fear, always with me. This relentless confusion in my mind. Gosh, the sun seems so bright, doesn't it?" She flared her nostrils and covered her face. "And when I look at you—"

"What?" his eyes begged.

"It's...nothingness. I can't do it anymore. I can't create.

I can't think. It feels like the world is closing in on me. Everywhere I look I see a room that's unfinished. I see my dreams being ripped away, and you and me growing further and further apart."

"I'm here. I've always been here," Joshua said. "We can deal with this together, but you won't let me help. You won't even touch me."

"It's never been like this before. It's never been this hard. But my mind is sick."

"Stop saying that. It's okay. It *will be* okay! I love you."

"You think that fixes anything?

"Every creative mind gets overwhelmed sometimes. Writers get writer's block. Teachers get bored. You think it's easy for me to carry everything? My firm? This house? You?"

She glared at him.

"I didn't mean that."

"Why'd you say it?"

He sighed. "Mary, it happens to everyone."

"Since when does a painter forget how to paint?" she asked, turning toward a rose to smell it and remind her senses of its sweetness.

"You haven't forgotten how to paint. I don't believe that, not for a second. Creativity comes and goes. It's a cycle. You just have to work through it, baby. It'll come back."

"You have this insipid notion that everything will always

just work out or get better. Well, it was better, for a moment, a very brief moment." Her mind flashed images of summers past. "But it came to an end. It's getting cold."

"Don't say that, my love."

"The leaves are turning," she continued, ignoring him. "The roads are damp with the rain. The flowers...bloom for the minute. But they will wither and die as well, and this garden will be empty."

"But it will be beautiful again. You know that. This is life, the circle of all things," Joshua said, raising her chin. "Why do you let this trouble you?"

Her eyes looked ghostly pale; her cheeks felt pushed in; a fever spread across her forehead. This gate, this perimeter, was a cell.

"Come inside with me," he pleaded.

"I can't handle that wretched smell. Not today."

"How long will you stay out here? How much longer can we stand to be apart like this? If we see each other at all during the day, you're distant. When you're alone, you're silent. Why do you push me away like this? I'm your husband."

"I know," she said, saddened. She knew she was supposed to love him, but it wasn't love that surged through her veins at this moment. Not love.

"Will you stay out here for the rest of the afternoon, then? I want to talk. I want to fix this. We can."

Mary pretended that she could feel a baby moving inside her. She had to protect it. She had to get it away from this confinement, this relentless drowning. "I'd like to go for a drive. Clear my mind. I should be back soon."

9

JOSHUA COULD SAY NO MORE with his words. He could do no more with his hands. He could wish no more with his heart.

Mary pressed her lips against his, and when she did, he felt a piece of him slip out. With a slow exhale, he searched his pockets for the keys to the car and gave them to her. Then she walked out of the garden.

Why did she distance herself from him? Why was she so afraid to tell him what lingered in her thoughts? He'd understand. He'd comfort her. He wanted to.

We're made to love, baby. Just come back to me.

Joshua's chest sank as she made her way toward the front of the mansion, through the brick walkway he had recently laid on the east side, and around to the porch which only needed a fresh coat of paint before it was finished. He hadn't intended for the mansion to take so long to be completed. He worked as hard and as quickly as he could to prepare a masterpiece for her. Was this uncreative force also plaguing him, slowing him down?

Mary's Pathfinder revved to life seconds later. "I love you," he whispered. He had work to finish inside. It was time to leave the garden and return. But something crawled across his untied boot just then. It moved slowly, as if with purpose and cunning. Joshua glanced down to find a black snake with spots along its back. The long creature's tongue tasted the air around his garden and draped its leathered skin along Joshua's ankle before dropping its belly once more to the ground.

Joshua knelt and stared into the snake's beady eyes. A union of white and red. His rough hands, beaten with blisters and poly, and tempered with the scent of his wife, reached into his rear pants pocket. His hand quickly emerged with a utility knife. He looked once upon the rose at the center of the garden bed, already beginning to wilt now that Mary's presence had gone, and then he turned toward the slithering, stained serpent and, with his thumb, pushed out the blade. In one swift motion, Joshua slid his fingers beneath the serpent's neck to hold it. With his other hand, he cut the creature in half.

5

HEARING JAMIE'S VOICE ON THE other end of the phone didn't calm Mary's sporadic nerves the way she wanted it to. But she hoped the familiar sound of it was a start.

"You sound sick, Mary," Jamie said.

"I'm not right, Sis," Mary answered, slurring her words. "I'm not all right."

"What happened? Did you and Joshua get into it again?"

A hush slipped in.

"I knew it. I knew it would eventually happen. You seem to fight a lot. We hardly ever hear from you anymore. How long's it been?"

"I don't know."

"I know you don't want to hear this, but what did you really expect? You uprooted your whole life for this guy. Does he know how fast he forced you to just change everything? What an overly ambitious—"

"It's not him," Mary shot back. "At least, I don't think it is."

"Oh, don't play into that scarred-little-girl mentality. Because that's how it starts. You blame yourself for one thing, and then give it a little time, and he'll be jumping down your back about something else. Even the littlest, stupidest things. Trust me. That's how these things happen."

"Not true," her sister's husband echoed in the background.

"Girl to girl," Jamie began, her tone taking on a more surreptitious nature. "Is it somebody else?"

"How can you ask me that?"

"Don't come at me all self-righteous," she whispered harshly into the phone. "You've never once thought about it?"

A long sigh from Mary's end.

"Well, forgive me for exploring a little. Sorry, I forgot you were so pure."

"I'm not. You're just terrible," Mary said between sobs. "I don't know how you live with yourself."

"You love me, admit it. Besides, it was just a one-time thing...that kept happening until I decided to end it."

"And have you?"

"Mom raised us better than that. Of course."

Mary saw right through. "You always were an expert."

"At what?"

"Masking the truth."

"Please, honey, I don't mask anything. You know, sometimes I'm as see-through as a teardrop. Can't exactly be burned at the stake because some people are just a little less intuitive, can I? Is it my fault they would rather hold onto their naïve notions of love?"

"Can your husband hear you right now?" Mary asked.

"Do you really think I'm that stupid?"

Mary couldn't believe the haughty pitch shaping her sister's words. There were dozens of abrupt conversations where Mary had been forced to hear how superior Jamie and her husband were as a couple. How united. But then again, it was the lies that held them together, she knew that. Having a child less than five months before the wedding had proven a heavy cross to bear and a constant inconvenience to her sister's selfish extracurricular activities.

The night turned misty, and the roads seemed to have adopted twists and turns she didn't recall. Mary glanced down briefly at the half-empty bottle of pills.

"I love him. I swear I love him, Sis," she tried.

"If that's the case, what's got you so worked up?"

Mary brushed aside a tear with the back of her wrist. "You've always been there for me."

"No one's ever confused me for the blessed Mother Teresa, but yes, I have. Still, I gotta be honest, ever since you met Joshua, you've been different. And since you lost the baby—"

"Don't!"

"I'm just saying I think it really took its toll, that's all."

"Am I that pathetic?" Mary asked.

"Don't get all insecure and self-deprecating. I'm stating a fact. A clear and simple fact."

Mary choked up.

"Listen to you. You're sobbing like a virgin on prom night. I'm starting to wonder if maybe it wasn't so good marrying this guy. Don't get me wrong, he's better than what I got. I mean, congrats and all that, but he took you away. From us, your family, your life, the city, everything you knew."

"We were never attached to any place, you know that."

"But like it or not, we used to be closer, you and me. I know I sort of drifted when I tied the knot, and...I just wish things could be different." A long pause spread between them. "I guess it's silly, really. I'm sorry. I shouldn't be putting this on you. It's your life. Maybe I've just always been a little, I don't know, jealous, before the tears and all the blah-blah-blah."

Mary sniffled and asked, "Why?

"What do you mean? You're my big sister. I copied you for, like, my entire life. But eventually, I had to redefine who I was. I met Robert, got a kid, the whole American dream, as you know. It's supposed to be beautiful, right?"

Mary could tell there was a deep sadness hidden in her sister's words, a transparency that hadn't been exposed in years. "I know that tone. Are you gonna file for divorce or something?" Mary couldn't believe she was actually more concerned for Jamie's marriage than her own.

"You kidding? Not until the fat lady sings," her sister jokingly replied.

"Robert's good to you. He loves you. Loves you both, more than anything."

"Why don't you take your own advice on this one? Look, why'd you call me? So I'd empathize with you? Tell you your husband's a scoundrel and you should get out while you still can? Stop living in what could've been. Look at *me*."

"I don't know what I wanted you to say," Mary confessed, noticing the tires pulling her vehicle toward the other lane. "I suppose...I just wanted to tell you I think I screwed up everything. I let it go too far. Things are gonna change for me, and I'm scared."

Jamie's ears must've buzzed. "You can't tell him, Mary. Don't you dare tell him. If he finds out...Oh, now you're just as bad as me. I can't believe I'm hearing what I'm hearing. You bad, bad girl." A sick kind of joy crept into her sister's voice. Mary pictured Jamie pressing her ear more forcefully against the plastic phone and curling up on the couch as if a new mystery were about to come on.

"No," Mary insisted. "I'm not having an affair. Oh no, I don't know what I'm doing."

"Well, what do *you* want, Mary?"

"I want you to tell me I'm just acting stupid, like a little girl. That I'll wake up from all of this and it'll be better."

"Wings never came, did they?"

Mary's heart drummed. The question stole her away from this moment, took her back so many years. She became that little girl again, anxious, afraid to be content in any one place.

She scratched her dream of escape into a wooden frame, carving out the future she wished for herself.

Her hands began to hurt. Her fingers turned numb from the pressure of the paperclip pressing into her skin and the bed frame. "I'll grow wings," she muttered.

"I don't know why you can't just be happy," Jamie said. "Go paint or something."

"It isn't that simple."

"Yes, it is. Find what you want and do it."

"What if I can't be happy? I'm scared. I don't know if I love him anymore. If I ever loved him."

"As if. He's still got his looks, and you're living in a mansion. How hard can it be? If you're not happy, you can at least pretend to be."

"It's an unfinished mansion," Mary said under her breath.

"Things could be a lot worse."

"What if I don't know how to be happy, Sis?"

"Is this about what happened in high school? I thought you eventually got counseling for that. Look, you've really got to get over your past, Mary. It's behind you. That's why they call it the past. Maybe it's like you told me, Joshua's good to you, or he's trying like a saint to make you happy."

"I should be happy. But there's this gaping question, this emptiness inside me I can't fill. I can't remember the last time I painted. I've lost it."

"I thought I lost 'it' the first few years I was married. Trust me, you haven't. Put it to you like this, if you could leave him, get out of the marriage free and clear, would you do it? Is that what you really want?"

Mary waited for an answer to come and deliver her. She wanted to loosen these rational chains. If she closed her eyes, bit down hard enough, screamed at the top of her cluttered lungs, maybe she'd have an answer. Maybe the bones in her back would shift, the stiff spine turning to clay. If she absorbed every breath and gripped the wheel like it was life itself and dreamed again, the feathers and cartilage might take shape next to her vertebrae and become the wings she had imagined for so long. She'd fly away from the country and the rains and drift into eternity.

"Mary...Mary...."

No reply.

Mary was lost in the gray of the clouds. The night was cloth around her changing skin. She was glowing, a fiery, rusted red. Behind her she glimpsed wings. They looked as though they'd tear the more they spread, the higher they carried her toward the moonlight.

But it wasn't real. It never was.

"Mary. Just think about it before you make a rash decision," Jamie said. "I know you. Have you skipped the pills?"

Mary quickly looked down at the orange bottle. "Why do you always jump right to that? I'm not an idiot!" *I took 'em, Sis. You'd be real proud.*

"Sorry. Relax, okay? You don't need to freak out just to feel alive. You and Joshua had a fight. It happens. Go back to the mansion. Take it from someone who's been there...You can learn to be content with him."

Silence again. And then Mary said, "He let me go."

"He gave you your space," her sister corrected. "But it doesn't mean he doesn't want you to come back. You called me, and I let you and your imagination have some fun. Now it's time to do what you're supposed to and play good wife."

"But I'm not good, Little Sis. I've got my spots, like any sparrow. I think I need to fly."

"Mary, you're not making any sense." Concern stumbled into Jamie's voice. "Are you drunk or something? Where are you? I can come to you."

"You're my little sister. I'm supposed to take care of *you*, right?" Mary whispered. "I love you."

"You don't get to say that. Not now! You're not acting like yourself. Where are you?"

"I am acting like me, actually. This is...the real me." Mary wrapped her lips around the open orange bottle and swallowed the remaining pills. "Love. It's such a funny, pretty word. That's how we're different, you...and I. I was never good at playing the part. I said the word, but I still don't know what it means. Maybe I just can't do it. I can't get better. Maybe I shouldn't be a mother."

Mary's ear rang from her sister screaming Robert's name

in a panic. "Miscarriages happen. For heaven's sake, stop crucifying yourself for something you had no control over."

"Is Dad there, Jamie? Tell him I love him. Kiss Mom for me."

"Dad's dead. Are you crazy? Tell me where you are now! Listen to me. If you get into an accident, I'm not burying you. I won't play this masochistic game again. I love you. I indulged you. But if you wreck this, I won't shed my tears, I swear. Go back to the mansion! Do you hear me! Go back!"

"You never believed in me and Joshua. Never. I can't keep hurting him, Sis. I can't keep hurting—"

Mary could feel the cell phone slipping from her grip. She was warm, her hands clammy and shaking as the drug spread inside her. Each blink was a desperate one. There was a black blur in front of her SUV, far off in the distance. The road was about to bend, and the visage came closer. She hadn't been checking the speedometer. She didn't much care.

The figure blended into the evening with the mist and fog. A flicker of moonlight reached down from the sky as the image appeared to split in two. Mary squinted, her eyes tense like a pulse. She could see someone walking on the side of the road. She imagined herself pulling over and asking the man to dance under the moon. The rain would provide such a soothing rhythm.

As the vehicle pulled her closer, the road bending more now, she gained some clarity. The man wore a trench coat and had on a black hat. Some of his long hair seemed to drip down his face, soaked from the rain. The only thing she could see perfectly were his eyes, a hint of red caught in each white orb. She knew it now, for certain. He was the figure who had stared at her from the road when she and Joshua came to the mansion for the first time. The man cloaked in black and fog.

In an attempt to avoid a collision, Mary cut the wheel hard to the left. The tires skidded across the velvet road. Traction slipped. The brakes gave out, sending her Pathfinder spinning into the guardrail. The metal from the hood of her vehicle ground against the metal of the railing, rust upon rust.

The screams from her sister on the other end of the still-connected phone call grew louder and more serious as the driver's side window exploded. Glass showered onto her jacket, and the door tore open, Mary's body hanging out. Frantic, she searched the road for drivers, for anyone. It was desolate and silent. The figure she'd almost clipped was nowhere. The rain, a violent fleet of arrows, cut into her hands and neck as her knuckles began to give way.

Her sister's pleas echoed from the floorboards now. Sooner or later, the rain would spill in and end the connection for her by corrupting the signal.

"Joshua," she cried, the cold of the night dragging across terrified eyes. She couldn't hold on for long. With a blood-curdling scream, Mary felt a tremor come over her hands. A very real fear invaded her chest, and her heart pounded. Her fingers began to slide until eventually she lost her grip and fell.

6

THE STAIN THAT COATED THE floor reminded Joshua of the brown residue he had seen on his teeth this morning. It was a cool-looking color on a floor, but it made him scowl at his reflection. One of the consequences of falling asleep late and waking up early in desperate need of too many cups of coffee.

Words like *gorgeous* and *breathtaking* should have been echoing off the walls, but they weren't. He'd sanded and re-sanded the floors, only to coat them thickly with a fresh brown layer. The entire process had been cathartic in a way, at least up until now. Joshua's hands, manicured with gook and dust and oils, were supposed to convince him that his labors weren't in vain.

But that's what this was, wasn't it? Vanity. After all, what newlywed couple needed a home so extravagant? What man in his right mind would be willing to invest his sweat, time, and soul into such a fractured existence?

"It isn't supposed to be this way," he muttered, wiping the edges of the floor. Joshua noticed a few sections in the wood where the grooves didn't sit as right as he wanted them to or a spot where he missed spreading the coffee-colored stain across the cuts and lines. Mary would notice; artists rarely missed such an imperfect thing.

Joshua wanted his bride here with him, now. He wanted Mary to call out his mistake. The thought of her not returning twisted his insides, and he hated it. But still there was a slow current of hope—a whisper within a dream that maybe he was capable of another beautiful mistake.

A soft, acoustic tune hummed in the background, but the guitar strings and the imitation drum score didn't reroute his burdened thoughts.

The room was almost finished.

Several more hours evaporated, like he knew the pungent smells of the mansion floors would, in time. But when? Joshua's concerted efforts of avoiding short glances at the clock across the banquet room weren't totally working. It was a demonic creature anyhow, as he saw it, always stealing precious breath away from the living.

He pulled open the fridge, which had nothing but old lunch meat and bad cheese in it and frowned, forcing the door immediately shut. Joshua checked his cell phone next. No messages. No missed calls.

Don't call her. Just wait.

But there was something different in her eyes. Something gone.

She'll come back.

What if...?

Joshua couldn't afford to deal in *what ifs*. Not now. He ran his fingers through his hair and breathed an exhausted sigh. Then he grabbed his keys and raced out to his car and into the storm.

7

MARY'S NECK HAD CRACKED IN various spots. She couldn't move it right. Her head throbbed. Her mind was drowning. Her eyes drank in the rain. Pink blood soaked into her white shirt. Her vision splintered as she blinked to find focus.

The night felt trapped all around her. No, *she* was trapped.

After struggling to breathe, Mary regained feeling in her face but nowhere else. Muscles still tense, bones adjusted. She hoped that if she could move her knuckles or twitch a leg, she might be able to rise out of this ditch and crawl back to the road. But as she gazed up the steep hill, she lost all ambition to move. Her eyes took in the sight of the stalled Pathfinder, its body warped by the violent collision with the guardrail. She heard the metal creak back and forth, the entire vehicle wavering on the edge of this nameless cliff, as if waiting to decide if it should let go so it could crush her completely.

She cursed under her breath. This backwards country road should never have been designated for travel, what, with all the twists and unexpected turns. And tonight, the bad weather.

But the weather was not to blame for her fall. Nor was it the slick traction that had victimized her tires. Nor was it Little Sis aching to convince her that walking out wouldn't give her the hollow shape of happiness she desperately needed.

"It's you," Mary quietly confessed.

Then she saw the mysterious figure in black sliding down the side of the cliff. How his hat managed to stay on his head during his clumsy descent, she didn't have a clue. But it was the one clear thing she could perceive in the darkness. Searching, she waited for those harshly lit eyes to seek her out.

She wanted to wail out a name, but she didn't know this strange figure. *Man. He's a man. Not a figure.* What was his name? Why was he here? Why now?

"Are you all right?" he yelled, his boots dragging into the hill's muddy, corrupted torso. As he snaked into the valley, an overwhelming fear knotted up her stomach.

"I said, are you all right, miss?" the man asked again. "Seeing you hit that guardrail scared me half to death, I gotta say. Can you hear me? Just hold on. I'm comin' for ya."

He had come to rescue her. "Where is Joshua?" she mumbled, the rain blending into her lonely tears. "Joshua?"

"No, miss. Name's Lucas Fisher," he said, sinking to his knees. "Can you move anything? Tilt your head? Flinch. Anything?" He had enchanting eyes. She must've been insane to think they could have ever been such a horrible shade.

"Where did you come from? I've seen you before."

Lucas carefully inspected her body, gently handling her crooked, broken legs. Mary's wrist had been caught between her body and a jagged rock. He winced, removing the rock and asking her to turn her wrist just slightly.

"I can't." Her stare never drifted from his. "Your eyes are like magic," she said.

"Okay, now I'm gonna lift your head up just a hiccup so I can get underneath. I'll be careful." Lucas eased behind her neck with one hand and, with the other, attempted to raise the rest of her.

She jerked when his hands agitated a protruding shard of bone. "Oh, it hurts like you can't imagine." Mary ground her molars. "Are you a doctor?"

"Not by trade, no. But I've got delicate hands, I promise. Always had a knack for taking away the pain. You just gotta be gentle with people. You gotta calm 'em down. Are you calm?"

"I'm trying, but it hurts so much."

"It's going to, Mary. It's going to. Tell me, can you move any part of your lower body?"

"I don't think so...H-how-how do you know my name?" she asked.

"Your wallet fell out of the car with you. I glanced at your license. Please don't alert the authorities."

"Oh."

He feathered her matted hair. The stars had abandoned her eyes and his. There was a blinding light that shined so furiously in front of her, but maybe paranoia was just hard at work playing a trick, guiding her toward a fearful doorway she wasn't ready to walk through.

All consciousness returned to the city, her home once upon a time. But Joshua wasn't there, and he wasn't here.

"Help me. Save me. Help me. Save me." The repetition was a jagged composition. Mary wanted to stroke his chin when her gaze captured his. With every blink, her face grew cold, her eyes opening and then closing again like untrusting misers.

"I think I'm...Lucas...I think...I can't m—*Joshua. Joshua!* I can't move at all."

"Shhh," he whispered, touching her lips. "Be still. It's just a dream."

Her throat quivered, and a fever burned behind her eyelids. *That* she could feel. But why could she not move anything below her neck? Had something broken beyond repair? She hadn't fractured any major arteries, had she?

"Can you do something for me?" Lucas softly asked.

"What?"

"Can you sing?"

"Why do you want me to sing? I've got such an ugly voice."

"It helps calm *me* down. I love music. I mean, doesn't everybody?"

"I suppose."

"Can I tell you a secret?"

"Yes," she answered with a shaky voice.

"I'm convinced one day music will save us all. Maybe even bring a person back to life, hallelujah!" He leaned in even closer. His hands were attempting a miracle, it seemed, the way they traveled and inspected her body. "Sing for me, won't you?"

Mary carried a tune she didn't even know existed. It was a tender verse that, despite her corrupted condition, new sensations spiked. She felt a blooming in her chest and then a heartbeat. Bones and muscles loosened in her arms. With his knuckles bent, Lucas slid his fingers down and across her frame. He began at her kneecap; it was a crushed, oozing mess. He slowly twisted the bones into proper place, aligning one leg with the other. Mary gasped in agony.

"Don't stop, Mary. Please, it will be over soon. I promise."

She bit down hard the next time she heard something make a splintering sound in the other leg. Was he breaking her or healing her? She didn't really know. But the song didn't cease. Soon after, a new awareness spread across her feet, and her toes suddenly flinched. A hidden smile returned to her face.

Lucas *was* restoring her.

Mary's shirt was torn from the fall, bits of flesh peeking through the wet fabric. Lucas delicately lifted the shirt and exposed her crunched spine. After kissing his fingers, he pressed them against her back. In seconds, feeling returned to her vertebrae. Mary could sense the chilled water tapping against her ribs. She managed to distinguish her heartbeat from the ringing in her ears, which she knew was Lucas's voice assuring her everything would be all right.

On the next blink, Mary watched a centipede tickle her belly with short needle legs. Lucas's peculiar hands finished bringing order to her battered joints and skin. He gradually stroked upward to her chest. His hands were careful and quiet devices, yet as he touched her, the nightmare she had endured long ago in a high school locker room once more ravaged her mind.

"He didn't hold you like I can, Mary. You must forget all that is past. I can take that pain you feel away. Just forget."

Mary wanted it to be so. She cried and let the tears roll down crimson red cheeks. His fingertips moved over her affectionately, resurrecting warmth that swept through her completely. The purple color in her neck turned white again, and when Lucas shut his eyes, he reinserted her splintered bone. It was a harsh, piercing slide, but the pain disappeared almost instantly.

"I feel everything now. I can move."

"Yes. But you must keep singing. Just sing."

Is the process hurting him? she wondered.

She swallowed. And in that moment she also bent her fingers, marveling at the sight of bruised and broken knuckles repairing in front of her very eyes. With a full breath, Mary rose from the unfiltered slush, stunned.

"How do you feel?" he asked her.

"Incredible. It doesn't make sense. I couldn't even move before, and you—" Mary stepped back as Lucas got up from the ground. "It's a miracle."

A grin stretched across his face.

"You fixed my body.

Lucas nodded.

"What are you? Some kind of devil?"

He chuckled.

"A witch?"

He shook his head. "I'm a musician, you could say. An artist. These woods are special, you see. Sometimes the trees can speak. Sometimes humans and animals interact. And on occasion, things are changed."

"Changed?"

"I've lived here a long time. I'll bet you didn't know that there is real magic in these woods. Most of them don't. Most aren't ready to know it."

Mary didn't understand him, but she believed him. After all, this stranger, this Lucas Fisher, whom she could have run over with her car, had just put life back into her. She had no choice but to trust him.

Mary started to shiver, so she rubbed her arms with her hands, still mystified that the cuts had vanished.

"It was fortuitous my going for a walk tonight, of all nights."

"I'm grateful the woods let you heal me." The reality of it all remained perplexing to her.

"It's a connection between the magic of these woods and the magic in our minds. The mind is a powerful creation, you know. Very powerful."

"I never knew it could literally heal a person," she confessed.

Lucas brushed her hair behind her ear gently. "Now you do." He held out his hand. "Let's get you out of this mess."

Mary hesitated.

"You're safe, Mary. Just take my hand. It'll be all right."

So charming and freeing were his words. Mary took his hand and with it, her first step.

"Follow me up now, back to the road," he said. "I can bring you home."

"Home?" she said, looking at him like a startled infant. A haze drifted over her mind. "I forgot the way back, I think." A chill slipped off her skin. "I'm afraid. Do you know a way back?"

"Yes, my dear. I know a way." Lucas marked her wrist with his lips just once and led her up the hill.

8

JOSHUA SWORE HIS STOMACH HAD turned to lead.
He parked his car on a small section of gravel right before the
road began to bend. It wasn't time to panic, but the damage
to the guardrail that blocked traffic from careening down the
sixty-foot cliff forced him to mutter brief, intermittent prayers
between his wary steps.

Where is her car?

The blackness of the night choked him. He spread his nostrils, picking up the rotting scent of a dead deer not far off. He
strained his eyes and caught a glimpse of the creature. Before
subjecting himself to the horrors his imagination toyed with,
the fear of what—sweet mercy—*who* lay at the bottom of that
cliff, he approached the unmoving animal.

The crunch of his work boots digging into the jagged stones
of the road was a corroded nail in his eardrums. The harsh
noise would soon plunge deeper into his disoriented subconscious. The closer he came to the dead animal, the sicker his
stomach turned. All his life, he'd never been taken by such
petty things. Death, after all, was a part of the mystery of life.

What reason was there to shun it? But here, now, things were not as they used to be. Things were not certain. Things were not in order.

A whisper lifted into the night just then. A mixture of this creature's pain and his. How similar and numbing both were. But on his next blink, Joshua came to realize there was no sound coming from the deer. *It's your own heart crying.*

He knelt on the ground and stroked the mammal's tan, stiff coat. Crimson syrup matted the torn flesh. The deer's belly had been sliced through and shredded. Joshua noticed an underdeveloped youngling lodged in the wall of a pink stomach. He peeled back some of the meat and exposed the frail, unborn thing. It was lifeless too.

Joshua pulled the unborn deer out of its mother and cut the umbilical thread with the utility knife from his back pocket.

"Speak to me," Joshua begged of the frail lives before him, his hands stained with their blood. He knew the request was mad, but still he hoped for an answer. Neither creature stirred. Their eyes held gray frost. "Sing the way you used to. I still believe in it."

In what, Joshua? In what?

"Love," he cried aloud, hoping the night could hear him. Hoping the blood that had cursed this mother and her infant to die could hear it, could feel the ever brittle vibrations in his throat. Praying to the sky for new warmth.

"It's almost finished. I almost finished our home. Can you hear me? Just a little while longer. Just a little while longer."

If anyone could see, they'd think him insane to be talking to a dead animal like it was his wife. Like it was Mary ripped open by some truck that didn't even bother to push her remains off to the side of the road. He both pitied and loved the creature. One of her eyes was shut, the other eye pulled back and reflecting Joshua's anguish.

Such a cruel fate. He smelled the caved-in chest. His tears weakened the vile stench. He dropped the unborn baby. Fatigued, he thrust his calloused hands beneath the mother and lifted her into his arms. His tongue wet thin, dry lips, and he sobbed with every step.

Joshua carried the deer toward the side of the road. It didn't matter that his cheek absorbed some of the black mess that had ruptured from her belly or that the mud caked along his wrists, mixing with the stain that was already there. The deer needed his love. Joshua's teeth tore at his bottom lip, waiting for the calm to come and steal away this disharmony.

But calm did not come.

Joshua found a fitting place to put her. The animal would sleep more softly now, away from the chaos of the storm. Dark dreams would seek her flesh out, surely. Perhaps the deer had run out too quickly without thinking of what it might mean. Perhaps she wasn't ready for what lay at the center of this foggy, paved stream of tar and dirt, its innocence left in the company of wild, whispering trees.

The pain multiplied, and Joshua's knees began to buckle. The harsh terrain cut into the denim cloaking his skin. Mist in the air caught his chin stubbles. A short beat lulled past him, and Joshua took steps toward the guardrail that had been torn through. But Mary's Pathfinder was not among the damage. *It should be here.*

Unless it wasn't her who had crashed. Unless he had imagined the frightful scenario and it was all awaiting his mind's inspection.

No, I felt it. I felt her fall.

He knew it so blindly that it was the only truth that existed. He saw Mary spiral out of control in his mind's eye, clearer than a dream. He saw her let go. He saw her crash at the bottom. The how didn't matter. The why wasn't important. All that remained was the unyielding reality that his wife....

"Don't," he told himself. "Don't let that horrible thought inside."

Joshua stood at the edge of the cliff. A piece of the road came loose, tried to drag him down with it, but he wouldn't be pulled. He remained a statue, staring down at the piles of mire and clay that the earth had borne.

Winter

1

MARY WOKE TREMBLING. Through a crystal blur, she studied her hands, checked her forehead. Temperature was normal. Then why was her heart racing? She noticed the unsettled veins lingering on the surface of her forearms. Curious. They strangely danced up and down, as if they found a dark rhythm hidden somewhere inside of her.

She heard the breathing of a man, but she didn't recognize him. More peculiar still: What was she doing lying next to him, in this bed, in this room? She had never been so reckless as to go to bed with a...

"Stranger," Mary's lips concluded. The word was claustrophobic behind her teeth. But when she uttered it, a chill sang through her bones.

Mary examined her garments: an elegant, white gown with an alluring cut at her sternum, enough to warm an imagination. Matching metallic bracelets fit tightly around both of her wrists.

Where did these come from?

What was a dream, and what was real? She began making a

mini list in her head, positive she had been wandering the coun-
tryside and the woods last night. At least, she was *mostly* certain
that it was last night that she had been driving. And then...

Memories flickered like dying candles in her mind. She
stepped out of bed, placing her feet on the floor. Mary felt the
uncomfortable slush of mud and sinking earth beneath her
feet, could sense the very souls of the rocks she had walked
over, as if she were there again. The sticks and dried-up roots
that sought to trip her in the isolated dark. *The weather was
terrible, wasn't it?* Yes, that was a fact. But where was she
coming from? Had she been speeding? Had she slammed her
head against the dashboard? Was that why the details were
so fuzzy?

Mary quietly glided across the open bedroom floor and
found the closest hanging mirror. "Get the facts straight, Mary.
Just get them straight." She tugged at her eyelids, massaged
her temples, smacked her cheeks, anything to jolt a memory,
to understand why she was here and who that man was in the
bed. Her belly felt empty. But not a hungry kind of empty; it
was a lacking, tired, painful sensitivity that spread through
her entire body.

"You took some pills last night." That was clear. If she
could get past that and the stumbling-around-the-woods bit,
perhaps she'd be a little closer to getting a grip. "Okay, you
took a lot of pills last night. And you wound up in bed with
some guy you can't remember." Mary frantically pulled at her

wiry hair and caught the shimmer of the bracelets once more out of the corner of her eye. "I hate bracelets."

The back of her mind spoke louder: *But they are exquisite, aren't they?*

"Must've thought I was pretty good." She felt a little bit of shame when that statement ran off her tongue. Dad would look down on her for this, she knew it.

Dad. Just call Dad. Ask him for advice. But a memory came all of a sudden, along with a gray picture. It was them—her and Jamie—standing, arms-locked, in a cemetery, listening to some droning preacher attempt to offer some encouragement when he claimed that Dad's failing heart was all a part of God's plan. Oh, and the hell that followed must have been a sick part of the divine plan as well.

Dad's dead. Oh no. Please no. She'd somehow had a lapse. Somehow had forgotten that he had died. That Mom had died. What was wrong with her? Mary blinked, and with a faint tear, she washed away another fragment of the past.

"The past is the past," she mouthed. "I do remember that." When she repeated it to herself, she heard a man's voice. Mary's gaze stretched across the ornate room, to the bed where the mysterious man lay, so soundly in his dream. It must've been beautiful, whatever he was dreaming about. *You told me that the past was the past. Of course, Jamie has been telling me for years, but when you spoke it to me...Yes, when I heard you say it, I believed.*

Mary wanted to shout her revelation, let it breathe out in the open for a bit; but what if he got angry? What if he had drunk too much last night and the booze hadn't yet filtered out of him? And what if there was still enough left to get him all levels of worked up? She was ill-equipped to handle that kind of confrontation.

What else was there? Had this creep sweet-talked her, promised her riches, to live in his fantastic house? Well, what if she didn't want it?

But then a startling reality shook her nearly off balance. Her eyes had found a diamond glistening like magic on her left ring finger. It had a white-gold band. How had she not felt it before? The diamond, a solitary stone, sat at the center of the flawless band.

"That man...is my husband?" she said, realizing that the statement evaporated off her lips more like a question.

The bedroom suddenly turned cool enough for Mary to see her own breath. She watched its frosty trail drift farther away from her, carried away by a breeze. Black curtains whipped; the doors leading to a balcony had been left open. The balcony. It was different yet familiar.

Her car. Of course. She couldn't be losing her mind, she just couldn't be. Her Path nder, rugged and run-down as it was, had to be parked outside in the driveway. It just had to be.

Mary glided from the spot in front of the mirror. In seconds she was looking over an immense courtyard that resembled a maze. The view from this balcony was wondrous. And the flutters in her chest subsided when she saw the vehicle parked exactly where she just now remembered she had left it.

Last night. Her mind paced. *Yes, last night.*

Her vehicle was in perfect condition. Why, then, did she have a hiccup of a thought that it may have been destroyed? She wanted control of this feverish polarity. Mary shuddered and fearfully locked her arms together, a breaking sensation draping her bones.

Off to one side of the courtyard, she saw a garden with an awe-inspiring collection of roses, petunias, and chrysanthemums, to name a few. Her eyes sparkled at the sight, but the unkind wind forced them shut again. Not for long. The pulse of the garden had a certain mesmerizing, undeniable quality. She longed to walk inside it.

Mary rushed out of the room barefoot. Down the long hallway she flew, confusion spreading through her organs like a tormented butterfly. If she were indeed married to the man in the bedroom, why did she not recall the ceremony? Had there even been a proper ceremony, or had she merely fulfilled his midnight lust?

Scratching her neck, Mary descended the stairs. She couldn't shake a familiar feeling, like she'd been in this house before, or one just like it. Come to think of it, should she even be calling this place a house? It was a mansion, if ever she saw one, and at the foot of the wide staircase, there were intricately carved marble birds. Crows. The detail in their wings and eyes and beaks was unparalleled. And the way their claws gripped each stone perch sent an eerie drip down her shoulder blades. The closer she gazed, the more she felt that the eyes were a startling black echo.

The garden.

She walked outside. Mary sought escape in the free, open space. Taking her first steps through the wrought-iron gate, Mary absorbed the sensitivity of the stone path and the grooves binding each pattern together. She was also aware of her knuckles cracking because she'd made a tense fist. But if she could just calm her thinking for a moment, maybe it was possible to get lost here in the sanctuary of the flowers.

How these blooming masterpieces had remained so un-stained by the encompassing winter world was nothing short of magic. How had the frost not filched their scent? How had the sleet not corrupted their emerald spines?

Carelessly, she tried to grip a rose by the stem, but a thorn pierced her thumb. It stung but only a little. Perhaps she'd grown up with a tolerance for pain. Mary lapped up the red sliver anxiously, noticing the cut was deeper than she first thought.

Closer to the center she moved, until at once she stopped short. As her nostrils filled with the fresh scents, Mary lightly touched a set of flowers thirsty for the attention of a sunrise. But there wasn't much light at all. An overcast sky hung above her, eclipsing the landscape.

Just then, a breeze chilled the front of her teeth. Her lips twisted into a frown. So suddenly it all changed. Mary quickly noticed that the very flower that longed for the sun's motherly glow began to wilt. The flower was dying, its petals tearing off like unwanted skin. In seconds, it was dust in her hands.

Startled, Mary turned around to gaze upon the rest of the garden. Pollen was choked the minute it drifted into the air. Petals slipped to the earth floor. Stems split in half. The bodies of these once precious things collapsed. Only thorns remained; a hideous miracle, really. What had caused it? It couldn't have been her touch. Her breath. Could it? Was it human contact that caused these beautiful creations to die?

"Enough. It can't be me." She stammered. "I don't understand it!"

She wanted to shed a tear for the petals withering at her feet or trapped in their potted coffins. These flowers were dead, and she needed to know the reason.

Mary ran out of the circle, shutting her eyes to banish the choking world from her thoughts. A vine caught her before the last step out, and she smacked her chin against the stone path. A curse ripped out of her as she bit down too hard on her tongue and the sharp taste of blood sprayed inside her cheek.

She tore her ankle free and raced to the Pathfinder and leapt inside, gasping for breath. But the keys weren't in it. She searched the visor and beneath the seats. Nothing. Panic seized her.

Mary stepped out and slammed the car door. She stared one last time at the house. What was it about the place that seemed to unhinge her? Her gaze drifted toward the balcony first, where she noticed a pair of eyes—belonging to the stranger with whom she had shared a bed—studying her.

No words were exchanged between them. The wind whipped her hair in every direction, an unkind and inhuman movement. Mary began to run as fast as her legs could carry her, repeating one word over and over. It was the only thing that stuck out to her clearly. A name. Joshua.

2

JOSHUA CUT HIMSELF TRYING TO hang one of Mary's paintings on the bedroom wall above the fireplace. He knew this was the most appropriate place to hang it, and the beautiful piece made the bedroom more inviting, if only for this moment. That was how he learned to view things now—in moments.

The blood trickling down his wrist reminded him he was still alive.

He'd lost track of the days. The nights. The painful afternoons sitting by himself. He remembered her name in prayers, but her face began to fade, and that reality was haunting.

The phone hadn't rung in weeks. Longer. He just assumed there was no connection at all anymore. Perhaps these woods, with wills of their own, had suffocated the union, like an infant in the womb strangled before taking its first breath. Most men, he knew, would soak their veins in liquor in order to subdue the terrible thoughts and the loneliness. But he wasn't most men. Some would undoubtedly run out and force their love to return, pressure her until she came to her senses.

But no.

The heat from the fireplace seemed incapable of making him warm regardless of how long he sat in front of it. One night, in the quiet, he had reached out his palms over the fire to let the feathered flame lick his skin. He only flinched, but he left his hands there until they scarred. A disfigured hand didn't seem to matter when compared to his loss.

Joshua slept on the floor often. It felt wrong sleeping in the bed without her. The leather couch in what should've been one of the living rooms had already begun to rip in certain places. Such weak material it was.

But he could never escape the regret that crawled through his blood. Maybe if he'd just begged her to stay, said the right thing, convinced her—forced her inside—she might not have rushed off. Maybe if he'd kissed her more passionately....

He missed her eyes too. And the precious smell of her body. But most of all, Joshua missed the way she sometimes pulled away when he leaned in close. Strange that he would long for such a silly thing.

As he stared into her painting, Joshua buried his face in his hands and began to cry. He had believed he was capable of lying here tonight in his bedroom. *Their* bedroom. But he was wrong. He clenched his bubbled hands into fists, almost pleased that the pain nearly gave him something else to feel. He imagined her walking toward him. He imagined his mouth pressed against hers.

But she was still gone.

3

BLISTERS POLLUTED HER FEET. Mary had been sprinting for what felt like forever. New snow blanketed the earth
as chilled breath was exhumed from her throat. Slivers of her
hair dabbed the sweat on her forehead. At last she could stop
running, but her spinal column had already begun to buckle,
sharp spikes of pain wracking her ribs.

She'd found her way back.

Still puzzling to her was the fact that she remembered
the way at all. How had she managed to cut through the
woods and paths of this hilly country without being hurt?
Without the moonlight or the stars to guide her? Why
had her chest not caved in? She had never been a skilled
athlete, so to assume it was normal for her body to endure
several miles of sprinting made little sense. But she had
made it.

All the things she had forgotten, but this place was not
among them.

Anxiety gripped her without warning. The darkness
breathed around her. A few blinks and she came to the

understanding that this darkness was inside of everything. It *was* the world around her. The darkness was life.

As she walked closer toward the mansion, Mary wondered where Joshua was. Would she find safety inside his great entry doors or hatred? What if he had forgotten her?

She uttered his name with a full breath: "Joshua." The short hairs on Mary's thin arms rose. A draft of wind moved across her skin, stroking her lips, scratching her teeth. It felt invasive but peaceful. *How can it be both?* She whispered Joshua's name a second time, and the pain that had wrapped around her spine moments earlier dissolved. Before she could say his name a third time, the sound of footsteps rang in her ear. She knew they were his. She didn't understand how she knew, but she did.

The patter had begun upstairs, in one of the far corners of the mansion, probably the bedroom. The floorboards creaked. She awaited his approach, listening eagerly as Joshua's heels struck the final step. He'd reached the foyer. He was so close now. She held her breath and touched the tree that sat at the center of the front yard. She felt the inner grooves, the section with a word carved into it. The tips of her fingers slid inside each letter, and at last she spoke the word aloud: "Once."

"Oh no," she said, a flood of knowledge—things she had done, said, felt—storming her all at once. "I'm not welcome here. He'll never love me. He'll never forgive me. He'll never... look at me the same."

She pinched her eyelids shut, knowing the action wouldn't stop the footsteps from drawing closer. "Joshua," she cried. But no relief came. The pain in her body returned, along with an even greater doubt.

In this grave hour, she had become a painting of the darkest shades.

She glanced down at her clothing, such tattered and unclean rags. Mud had splattered the once brilliant white. Her hands were heavy weights at her sides. Fear captivated every pulse. *He's going to hate me. I know he's going to hate me.* She never should have left the other garden. Why had she wandered here? This was the past. And the man in her bed—*what is his name?*—was her present.

The footsteps boomed louder. They could not be stopped. They sounded like they belonged to the body of a hulk. A hulk that was coming for her.

Her shoulder blades scraped along the willow tree, where her hands had first trembled. That word. That godforsaken word. She knew in the depths of her being what it meant, but could it be undone?

Closer. Closer still those terrible footsteps.

"I have to fly from here."

She collapsed, and as she did, something like a splinter began to shred her back apart. It tore out of the left side of her, beneath the shoulder blade. There had to be blood, but she didn't have the guts to dab her fingers into the new wound.

The pain enveloped her shaking body. Joshua finally uttered her name.

She lay perfectly still, terrified of what he might do to her if he found her. The pain moved, and through the darkness she could see a shadow looming over one half of her. It dangled slightly above her face, but it came from behind. Her back. That sharp, twisting sensation had produced a disfigured wing. With shock-lit eyes, she watched a feather come loose and drift away. The wind had stolen it, carrying it all the way back to the porch, where Joshua stood like a weathered, beaten gravestone. The flickering light behind him created his shadow, something harsh reaching out to blend with the darkness.

A tear slipped down her cheek. She trembled. *Did I actually grow a wing?* It looked thin, showing more bone than feathers. It hung there limp, waiting to be used. But where was the other wing? If she were to accept that a wing had just ruptured out of her back, why was there only one?

Mary strained, crawling across the finished driveway, hoping she'd make it to the surrounding bushes before Joshua noticed her. It was odd. She wanted to see him. To be held. She wanted him to make sense of everything, and she wanted to ask him how she'd ever slipped away from his mansion. Their mansion, once. She'd lost her step, but she also found her way back. Didn't that count for something?

But that cursed, terrible word was too real for her to put it out of her mind. It wouldn't let her go. She was the word at the heart of the willow tree. Such a miserable, ugly thing.

Mary had enough strength to force the wing back inside her body. She reached her right arm around to where the opening was. Still-wet blood slipped out of a narrow incision. Remarkable and scary.

She shivered. Snow sank into her neck and chest, eventually melting. Joshua walked down the porch steps, noticing the footprints her feet had made. But he stopped still, standing in the middle of the lawn. Waiting. Silent.

Mary was desperate for understanding and true knowledge. Just what had happened to her? And why couldn't she fully remember? How long had she been gone from here? How long exactly?

Mary eyed him, breathless. She read the heartache in his stare, sensed the stuttering beat in his chest. And though she feared his wrath and bitterness, neither was on display. He searched the darkness, looking for *her*, she was certain. But she was hidden well. Mary wasn't ready. She couldn't face him so unclean and ruined and with a deformed wing. She couldn't even wrap her mind around that last part. No matter how many times she pinched herself, Mary knew there was no waking up from this.

Joshua moved again. He walked to the tree, pressed his hands against the word carved there. Mary felt the pressure of his fingers drift along her bones then.

How is this happening? How is any of this happening? Joshua was a normal man, wasn't he? He didn't possess any power or supernatural ability. But when he kissed the tree and said her name—whispered that he loved her—she was no longer certain of anything.

He dried his tears with his sleeve and toyed with the metal on his ring finger. He didn't seem to care that his teeth chattered or that his ears had turned red. White breath circled his face like smoke. Still he stayed.

But she didn't move. Her pulse shivered in her neck as he said her name again. Joshua's voice left her nearly paralyzed. More tears were spilled. His tears did not belong here. Neither did she.

The wing still felt peculiar sliding around in her back. Like it was getting comfortable there. The other wing didn't come. She wasn't sure if it ever would, but right now, she knew she had to get away from here. She wasn't ready for the answers. She wasn't ready for any of this.

When Joshua turned around to walk toward the mansion, Mary sprang to her feet and started running. Some blisters on her heel popped. She winced but didn't slow. The pain spreading in her toes was nothing. The icy snow igniting her skin was nothing. Their love was...

Don't, she begged her conscience. *Don't say it.*

"Nothing."

9

WHEN MARY RETURNED TO THE place where she'd woken up, the man who had slept beside her was waiting for her, sipping a glass of wine. Fine, classical music filled the room. She entered cautiously. Her hands still trembled, and a bit of mud remained on her cheek from a fall she suffered a few miles back. Mary counted the seconds. She couldn't catch her breath.

"Where were you?" the man asked.

Her eyes wandered then came back and met his. She still could not recall his name.

"I asked you a question."

"I went for a run," she said quietly.

"A run? In the middle of winter? Dressed like that and barefoot? It's getting worse."

Mary ignored the cruel shivers.

The man took another sip of his wine before rising to greet her. "Well, I'm just glad you made it safely back to me, sweetheart."

Sweetheart? She didn't like the way his voice made that

term of endearment sound. The word slithered out and carried poison with it.

He stepped toward her, and she leaned back against the door. She preferred the distance. He stroked her chin. "There, there. You look as though you've seen a ghost. Don't you recognize me?"

She didn't answer.

"I know that look. I saw that same look when I watched you in the garden this morning. Like you don't belong. Like you don't know who you are."

Mary blinked, a lot. Her nostrils flared. Her hands touched the door, and she could feel a draft coming through.

"Mary, it's me. Lucas."

"Lucas?" she repeated, puzzled still.

"Your husband."

"My husband," she said, reminded once more of the ring that clothed her finger.

"My goodness. I knew I never should've let you leave again. All this time...I'll have you know, it was always against my better judgment." He paced the floor. "It's been snowing since you left. Are you trying to get sick? The cold temperatures aren't good for you, especially considering...your condition."

"Condition?"

Lucas spent a moment collecting his thoughts. "The accident, Mary. You haven't been well for some time. From your fevers to your memory loss. Amnesia. I've been waiting for you to regain your true self, all of you, for a long time. Only I and the best doctors have taken care of you, but they said you would heal eventually, if I let things simply play out."

"The accident?" She now remembered the accident, a part of it. She felt a sharp pain twist through her leg, her arms, her wrist. "How long has it been?"

Lucas sighed and kissed her cheek. "Three years."

The ground had to be shaking under her feet. In the next few blinks, this massive house would come crashing down upon them both and she'd finally wake up. The wing in her back would vanish and the wound would shut up. And this fiend would be silenced.

Lucas reached for her hand.

"Don't touch me," she spat.

"Why are you so hostile?"

"Lucas?" she said, the name still very much a stranger on her lips. "Is this a trick?"

He shook his head with dim eyes.

Three years? How had so much time passed? Could seasons last like this? Could a winter endure so long? Her mind swam.

"I knew the risk when I took you as my own. I understood that your memory might come and go. You hit your head so hard in the crash, Mary. The trauma, the loss of blood. It was the hardest thing I've ever had to bear. But what I knew more deeply than that reality, what held me together, was that I was certain you would be mine. Whether you could remember me or not, my longing for you would not change."

"It's still a blur."

He kissed her forehead. "You're so very precious to me. Try to remember, won't you?"

"Remember," Mary murmured. "The crash. It was raining. I saw a man in the road. Then I fell. So far. I hit my head and ev-erything went black." She paused, waiting for her subconscious to trigger more violent flashbacks. But nothing else came.

"You don't recall the ambulance ride?" Lucas asked. "Your sister, Jamie, panicking because she thought she'd lost you? Or the several weeks you spent in physical therapy before I demanded that you be seen by only the best, here, where you're safe? I was here, with you, loving you through it all."

"We got married?" She forced herself to say it. She'd read books that told her to speak things into existence; that, if you could make yourself believe it, whatever reality you believed in would come to pass. *Just believe*, she told herself.

"Yes. Three years ago, darling."

"But Joshua—"

"Who?"

"Joshua. I know him. I...loved him." Mary tried to reconcile that truth with Lucas's truth. But they could not coexist. "He owns the mansion several miles away. The one that was close to being condemned, about ready to be torn down, I imagine. But it looks...breathtaking now. I don't know how he did it."

Lucas smirked and turned his back. "I had hoped...Mary, I can't believe we're going down this road again. I can deal with you not remembering it all. I can deal with the distance between us. I can deal with your fevers and your emotional stirs. But I refuse to indulge these ridiculous illusions anymore."

"Illusions?" she said, tense. "I was there! I was there tonight."

"And where is *there,* exactly? Does it have a real address, or is it only in your mind? This here is the only mansion out in these woods. Other houses perhaps, but nothing like this. I don't know where it is you go all the time, but I can be certain that it isn't to any other fantasy mansion."

Did he realize how shortsighted he sounded? She wanted to leave this room. She needed a shower.

"You don't believe me," she said, defeated. "You really don't believe me."

He crossed his arms. "I'm sorry, but we've discussed your nightmares before."

"It isn't a nightmare. It's real. I'd show you, but I don't see the point."

"You can be so defiant at times. Maybe this game feels new to *you,* but it isn't to me. And, to be honest, all this talk of a Joshua has gotten old. If you're trying to get my attention, you don't need to invent mysterious men and ramble on about mansions that don't exist!"

"Ramble on? Is that what you call it, dear husband?"

"Don't take that tone with me, Mary! I'm merely expressing my frustration at the situation. It's been hard for me...seeing you like this, watching you deteriorate."

"Well, I apologize if my memory loss is an inconvenience for you." Mary shoved him aside and ran toward the stairs, but Lucas stopped her short.

"What is that?"

She knew his eyes were studying her. She turned around. "What is *what*?"

"That cut in your back. Below your shoulder blade. What happened to you?"

"I fell, that's all."

"It isn't infected, is it?"

She ran upstairs. "Don't worry. It's nothing."

5

MARY WASN'T IN THE SHOWER long before Lucas knocked on the door. It was cracked open slightly, the steam creeping out as he moved in. "Is it too late to ask for forgiveness?" he asked.

No reply.

"I realize I shouldn't have taken my frustration out on you. My reaction wasn't fair."

"No, it wasn't." She let the hot needles invade her body.

Lucas pulled off his shirt and unfastened his belt, letting his pants fall to the marble floor. "Mary, you mean the world to me. Don't you know that?" Pulling off the remainder of his clothes, he put one foot in the shower to join her. "Seeing you like this is wearing on me, that's all. I'm not a monster."

She faced the wall, the water trickling down her spine, dripping into the cut. He shouldn't be here. She didn't want him here. "You're making me uncomfortable," she said. "Please get out."

"Relax," he whispered, kissing the section where the flesh split. A wing moved underneath her skin.

"I'd like to be alone. You should go."

"Am I so horrible? My only crime is that I want to be with you." His hands turned her around so they could face one another. He gazed into her eyes.

"I don't believe you. I don't know what to believe anymore. Nothing makes sense."

"Why would I lie to you?" He pulled her close. Their bodies collided, and the water passed between her chest and his.

"Why don't I recognize this place? Why can't I remember marrying you?"

"I don't know. The universe can be cruel sometimes. But I knew this wouldn't be easy. Romance never is."

His words loosened her veins, turning her blood cold. She closed her eyes and rinsed the shampoo out of her hair. Then she finished washing the soap and dirt from her back as Lucas put his finger inside the tear in her shoulder. His fingers squished around. A tingling sensation stuttered through her abdomen and lower back. Her thighs moved beneath a quivering center.

"What are you doing? I'm fine," she said, denying to herself that his hands stimulated her. "You shouldn't touch it."

"What is it?"

Vulnerable and unsure, Mary blinked hard, and the wing climbed out, unfurling around their bodies. Part of the shower curtain tore. What stunned her most was Lucas's reaction to the wing. He wasn't disgusted. He didn't think she was a mutant. Instead, he moved inside. He stared into her eyes as if he actually loved her. Her sickly wing twisted around his back muscles. She could feel them too. It was a calming sensation. Maybe the sensation was the love she swore she had never believed in.

They kissed passionately for a long moment.

"It's beautiful," Lucas whispered into her mouth.

6

SHE'D SPENT THE NIGHT IN Lucas's warm arms. The passion they experienced was the most strangely beautiful thing. Transcendent. A harmony, even, she could not get out of her mind. And she didn't want to.

His left hand reached over her, covering her breast, the sheets doing the rest. He lay there, content in his sleep, while she simply stared at the ceiling, marveling at the intricate patterns and the way the walls and decorations came together without any effort at all. The way things never used to work.

She brushed aside her hair and glanced at Lucas. New confidence ravaged her. A trust. He moved in his sleep just then, and she noticed a vein in his hand dance above her milky skin. Flesh never looked so smooth. A smile twisted her lips. And for the first time since she'd woken up beside him early yesterday morning, she felt like her world was about to fall into place.

She didn't care about Joshua or the mansion Lucas convinced her existed only in her dreams. She disregarded the journey, the endless running toward an unknown destination. *But I was there*, she thought. *I was there.*

It didn't matter. The past was the past. Maybe she'd never reached the mansion she claimed was there, tucked away in the woods like this one. Maybe she'd never seen Joshua or his wretched willow tree.

Mary let go of the snapshots of her past. She didn't want to war with them anymore.

Gently, she dragged Lucas's hand off her chest and placed it beside her on the mattress, kissing it first. Stepping out of bed, she searched for her nightgown and put it on. She bent over to scratch an itch on her ankle, and when she did, she caught her reflection in the mirror on the other side of the room. She walked toward it, marveling at what she saw. A second hole had appeared in her back. A new opening that looked as though thin fingers, cartilage and tendons, were crawling out of it.

She whispered, "It's a second wing."

Mixed with the shock was gladness. A joy that had been planted at the root of her entire being. She flipped the hair away from the opening, and the flesh surrounding it squirmed. The wing was alive. With shut eyes, she envisioned it, along with its counterpart, reaching out and expanding. In seconds, each wing fluttered out in a fantastic way. Exposed. Free. Once unfurled, her wings eclipsed any artificial light in the room, encompassing her in the shade of their splendor.

Neither wing appeared sickly. Both possessed full feathers and an undeniable, majestic color that she swore did not even exist in the spectrum. Mary wanted to wake Lucas. But she didn't. Instead, she concentrated the muscles in her back, and with gritted teeth she drew the wings once more into place inside her body. The feeling was peculiar but also pleasurable.

Again, she tried to extend them. And again, the wings spread out, unraveling the air behind her. There was a sudden *whoosh* and then no sound at all. How seamlessly and rapidly the extension of these muscles, these organs, whatever they were, occurred. Perhaps even more remarkable was the fact that such a thing happened at all. What made a human being suddenly develop wings?

"It doesn't matter how it happened. They're incredible. They're strong. Beautiful." That was the way Lucas described them when he touched the opening last night as the warm water from the shower head splashed against their faces and the union of their bodies. *Beautiful.* Like wonder. Like angels.

She shut the wings up a second time, barely capable of holding in her excitement. Like tasting a piece of fresh fruit for the first time. She felt whole and complete.

As she turned around to walk toward the bed where Lucas still slept, she felt a swelling in her forehead. It came upon her at once. But she ignored it as nothing more than startled nerves.

Mary painted for the next few hours on the balcony

outside their bedroom. She wondered if Lucas would ever wake. Perhaps he was still bound by a dream. A dream, she imagined, similar to the one she painted. It had a magical, breathtaking color to it. With trees and flowers. She gazed at the trees as they swayed. She imagined them with powers. She didn't recall where this idea came from or why, but it lingered. *The trees have power. The woods have power.*

Mary included a grand garden in the piece. This garden could be more real than any one on earth. It wouldn't die. It couldn't wilt or hurt. She dipped the brush into a pale blue and began adding shades to the sky. With every stroke, she imagined getting lost inside the image, like Lucas in his dream. She was safe in her created, cloudless heaven, protected by its color and warmth.

It was almost complete.

A few of the flowers needed another splash of vibrancy in their petals. And the garden's front gate could use an angel or two to shelter the flowers. She added the heavenly beings more out of superstition than because she believed they possessed any real power.

The painting looked so real by the time she was done that she half expected herself to touch it and be sucked into its landscape. But when she blinked, Mary realized how silly the thought was.

To her surprise, she then started sweating. That feeling from earlier had returned. With the back of her hand, Mary rubbed her forehead and cheeks, forgetting her hand still had some paint on it. She probably looked like a clown now. What she felt like, however, was a clown with a fever. But it couldn't be a fever, could it?

Mary got out of her chair and stepped away from the canvas. She blinked, and the scene before her suddenly started to blur. She tried to swallow but couldn't. She turned toward the bed. Lucas wasn't there. She turned back to look at the afternoon sky, but it wasn't there. Instead, there was only darkness. It had changed in a split second. But how was that possible? Day didn't just become night. Clouds didn't suddenly disappear and become stars, did they?

The heat from her forehead moved toward her belly, making her think she might vomit. But it wasn't vomit; it was blood staining her shirt. Scarlet blotches soaked into the material at the center of her, ruining the pure fabric. Mary gasped. What was happening to her? With every breath, the magic faded more. She took another step toward the bed. "Lucas? Lucas!" she called out in a panic.

Where was he?

Mary was afraid. She had to know what was wrong. Her memory was a twisted metal cage filled with jagged edges and no center. "Lucas! Where are you?" She took another step, and her vision flashed white then black. Then blurry once more. The bed seemed so far away. So very far away. Before the sound in her eardrums cut out, Lucas's faint breaths invaded the room.

He spoke her name as she collapsed on the floor.

"Lucas," she gasped. "Lu...cas."

Through the blur, she saw him drop down on his knees, placing his hands beneath her head. She could make out slightly how he kissed her forehead as he held her. But when he looked into her eyes, she saw someone else—a man with a hat and an unsettling grin. The clothes Lucas had on had changed. He now wore a tattered shirt and a long trench coat that snaked around her legs. A lengthy, chipped nail dragged across her lips.

"Lucas?"

"Yes, my Mary," she heard him say, the sounds muffled. "What is it?"

"Something's wrong. I don't feel right." She dabbed her stomach. The smell of copper clouded her nostrils. "My baby. I lost my baby." A tear slipped from her eye as she said it. "I lost...Help me. Please, won't you help me? I can't remember it all. I want to remember." An image of the night of the accident stormed her mind. She had fallen. She was sinking in the mud and rain. He was there to witness the fall. Lucas Fisher, the drifter who had touched her and healed her.

He laughed a breathy laugh. "Forget, my sweet. Forget! Don't you see? I *have* helped you. I gave you a gift. The transformation took some time, but finally you accepted it. The pain will stay with you for a little while. It will feel like torture, but that'll go away...in time."

"You did this to me? But how?"

"There is power in these woods, Mary. Unimaginable, unfathomable power." He paused, eyes slanted. "I control these woods. My power exists in the trees, in the air, all around us. So much of this world can't see it, can't know it. But *you* can. You experienced it the night you fell, didn't you? Isn't this what you've always wanted?"

She swallowed hard.

"I set you free, baby."

Mary shook her head. She shut her eyes. Joshua was there in her mind, painting the walls of his mansion. She opened her eyes to Lucas's haunting grin. She shut them again, and Joshua put the finishing touches on a family room. Their children would play there. They'd be happy. Her lids peeled back again, and this time, Lucas's shadow grew and dripped over her. In that moment, she could not be sure if it was the light playing tricks on her or if what she saw—Lucas looming over her in a new bat form with torn, mutilated wings and fangs that dripped red—was real.

"What are you?" she asked, her hands slick with sweat. She tried to crawl away from the creature, to draw closer to the mirror so she could see him for real, if her eyes didn't spite her.

"I am your beloved. And you are mine now. Don't squirm. You'll only make it worse."

"I thought you were—"

"What? You thought I was what?" he growled. "Your savior?" He cackled. "I saw something in you that I liked. I always liked you, Mary. But he wanted you too."

"Joshua?"

"Yes," he said with a snarl, his hot breath consuming the air around her face.

"He does exist."

"Over the years, you'd think of that wretched fool, cry for him. So I let you out to see if a hurt, broken thing like you could ever find her way back. I did what I never allowed the others to do. I let you roam the woods. I let you experience that precious love lost, and it worked, you see. You always came running back. I can't explain our connection exactly. But it's real, I can promise you that. Our romance is more real than anything that pathetic man ever gave you."

Her eyes were heavy. Confusion clouded her consciousness. Mary felt hate crawl up her gut. "You deceived me. You *are* a monster!"

"Am I? I gave you your heart's desire. You wanted wings. You wanted real love. I am lord of these woods. I am all you need."

She crawled, scratched at the floor with her nails. *Get away from me*, she thought.

"My true form frightens you, doesn't it? Well, soon you will come to know me and my form. Like your art. Like poetry. Our souls have intertwined." His shadow engulfed her body.

"You're changing too, Mary. Even now, I can see your form becoming more. The change is taking over."

"Take it away, Lucas. Take it back! I don't want it anymore."

"That's not how it works. I will not take it back. We are one now."

With desperate hands, she pulled herself toward the mirror. Strength was leaving her. Her vision splintered and blurred even more. Sweat pooled under her drooping, blackened eyes. At once, the holes beneath her shoulder blades began to rip even more, the tears in the flesh expanding and stabbing down her spine. She cried out.

Lucas, the black bat in a trench coat, spoke again. "Joshua wanted you weak. He held you back! He imprisoned your true nature."

"I hate you," she said. "You...lied to me." She caught the distorted reflection in the glass. Squinting, Mary saw the hideous bat hunch over her shuddering body, his large, scaly legs and gnarled claw feet crushing her. There was a crunching sound, and the wings crept out of her, slowly this time. It was strange; they were not like wings at all but more like limbs from an exhumed corpse. She no longer loved them.

"I never meant for this. I didn't know." The colors in her eyes reflected darkly in the mirror. And so did Lucas's blood-red glare. His ugly snout unloosed a crippling slur.

"You don't have to fight it this much. You are so beautiful,

Mary. You were always beautiful to me. Here you will find your place among my brides."

The door that led to the hallway suddenly opened, and three winged creatures slowly pulled their bodies closer. One of the creature's ribcage was exposed, pieces chewed off like a vulture had picked at her flesh for several hours. The middle creature's skin dripped lazily off her cheek bones. She looked old, with gray hair and black teeth. The last had enough strength to climb the wall and skulk closer. Mary heard her breathing, whispering in some language she didn't know. This last bride frightened her the most. Long, black hair cascaded down scaly shoulders. A feather torn loose from one of her mutilated wings had been shred in certain parts. Ice-blue veins blistered a wrinkled forehead. Drool bled out of a gaping mouth, with fangs and a tongue that searched the air.

"She is one of us," they all chanted together.

"Yes," Lucas hissed.

"We...were pretty once too, weren't we? Like this pretty one?" the creature on the wall asked.

"Be still, my sparrows."

"Let us get her first, pretty, pretty please," the one with the exposed ribcage begged. Her protruding bones scraped against the floor, creating an eerie, tempting sound.

"No," Lucas said. "She is mine. She is...special."

The brides shrieked, flapping their wings in protest. "Give her to us! We have not fed in so long. Must you be so cruel?"

Lucas clutched the weakest by the neck and squeezed her throat until her eyes started to pulsate. Mary feared what might happen to her if she continued to question Lucas's plans.

At once, she felt the ground tremble. Her ears took in the vibrations in the floorboards. Footsteps. Dragging bodies. Flapping wings. It was so loud in the mansion now. She could only surmise that more of these grotesque beings were coming. How many more? She didn't know. Had they always been here, invisible to her?

Lucas dropped the dead bride from his grip. Her body squirmed some, her wing stuttered on the floor, but in seconds she died. The others ate her flesh.

The sound was closer now. Mary's breaths grew shorter and more desperate. She had to get out. One of the creatures clawed at her ankle. Her fingernail was a rusty talon scratching at flesh that already began to turn. *What will I become?* Mary wondered.

"Mary...Mary," the two creatures moaned in unison, their jaws satiated for the moment. But she knew they wanted her too.

Closer. Closer. The noise. The footsteps shook the floors, the walls, the ceilings. She imagined all the creatures attacking her, clawing at her until there was nothing left but *her* ribs, *her* rusty, misshapen claws.

"Come, my winter sparrow, and take your place as my new bride." She hated Lucas's slimy voice.

"I'll never be yours!" With all of the strength Mary

possessed, she lifted herself off the floor and swung her fist into Lucas's hairy snout. His fangs cut her knuckles when she struck him, but the blow shook him off balance. He stumbled back, shocked and furious. Now was her only chance to escape. She glanced, petrified, at the dead life all around her. The horrifying mutations had reached the bedroom at last. With tears in her eyes, she raced for the window and dove into it. Glass shattered and sliced the flesh of her arms, which was becoming scales, and she descended.

Her memories returned. She was hanging from her car door. She was weightless. Breathless. Afraid. She let go.

At once, Mary felt movement in her back. And before her body crashed onto the ground, her wings unfurled, and she glided into the strange woods.

7

MARY THOUGHT ON MANY THINGS as she flew toward Joshua's mansion. She thought of her youth, of Little Sis, how awkward growing up had been, and how unprepared she was for these wings. She thought of that horrible boy groping her breasts in a locker room. Thought of what she wanted to do to him. *He* was the bat. *He* embodied those creeping monsters on the bedroom floor and on the walls and the ceiling.

She thought of the wedding. It became so clear. She had been a fool to ignore it before, even though it crept up from time to time. How long she'd been locked away in Lucas's false haven, she still didn't know for sure. It was summer in her mind, and she let Joshua kiss her. She could taste his sweet breath. She swore she could also taste the certainty of their love on his lips, what *she* had always been lacking. It didn't matter what Lucas had drilled into her brain; Joshua loved her. Lucas's mansion had blinded her to that reality.

Mary cut through the moonless sky, flying over the trees and between them. She heard them wailing. She heard critters stirring about below. She heard whimpering wolves somewhere. But she didn't fear any of it. She was close to Joshua's home. A few more blinks and she'd arrive.

But suddenly, there were other wings in the air. She heard them swoop and flap, and she listened for gross, disturbing breathing. Mary looked back. Lucas. She didn't have much strength left, she knew, but what little she possessed, she used to fly faster.

He gained. He'd bring her back to his world. She didn't like it there. She didn't want to go back. She couldn't, not now, not after the knowledge she had tasted. It was as if a thousand memories crashed in her subconscious at the same time, and her will was capable of processing it all.

She remembered. She remembered everything.

Joshua's mansion waited. It was in sight. Mary began her descent, and as she did, Lucas clutched one of her wings with his talon. She fought mid-flight, but his strength was too powerful. With a growl, he tore into the wing. It split like fabric. Mary shrieked, the pain racing down her ribs. He lunged for her throat as they dropped faster and faster toward the earth. At last, they crashed like thunder. Their bodies formed a crater in the dirt, landing at the foot of the long driveway.

"Joshua!" she screamed at the top of her lungs.

Lucas shook his head, recovering from the impact, and quickly rushed to silence his victim. His mammoth right talon elevated her off the ground, and with his other talon he covered her mouth. The stink of his hair put her stomach in knots. Mary

WINTER SPARROW | 147

bit his forearm, and he cursed, slugging her hard. She flew into one of the trees. But the pain didn't kill her. She got up and raced toward the porch, shouting her true love's name.

Lucas flew into her, and as he did, his shape changed back to a man. The tall figure with a black hat and yellow teeth held her in a viselike grip.

Her vision returned fully. She called out to Joshua once more.

Lucas still had use of his fangs. He bit into her torn wing, chewing the flesh of it with hungry eyes. He then spit at her. "I made you beautiful. I gave you a new life. And this is how you repay me? You return to him like a frightened little whore!" His mouth twisted into a demonic smile as he ripped the wing out of her back. Blood sprayed his coat.

Mary dropped to her knees, moaning as new pain rushed into her bones. She saw Lucas toss the wing and slowly watched it wither on the grass. Tears sank into her cheek cold. Her other wing still fought to move, to attack her enemy. It flapped helplessly in the air. His vile grin mocked its infant strength.

"Joshua," she whispered. "Please."

"It's too late, Mary." Lucas reached down to grab her when the front door creaked open.

He was still.

She was still.

Joshua's footsteps made them both uncomfortable.

"Who are you?" Joshua asked.

"You know who I am!" Lucas seethed, taking hold of his prize.

"Not you. The girl."

"It's me, Joshua." Mary wiped her face and shivered. He'd recognize her, wouldn't he? "Don't you see me?"

Joshua walked down the steps of the porch. He was still handsome, but his eyes and his face now glowed a brilliant white. He watched her shake, studying her. She wished she were wearing something more becoming, not this ruined beggar's cloth. She didn't even have the right shoes. And the bracelets on her wrist cut into her veins.

"It's me," she said again.

"What is your name?" Joshua asked.

"Mary. You know me. We were married. We *are* married."

Joshua shoved Lucas aside and gave Mary a cursory glance. "I do not know you. Why are you here to bother me, widow?"

"I am your wife!"

"No. I see no bride of mine here. I see only a widow in rags, with a broken wing. You've come here to wake me out of a dream, have you? Is your ghost here to torment me?"

Lucas grinned. She noticed the satisfaction flickering in his eyes. It was startling to see the beast once more disguised as a man.

"Joshua, you're talking like a madman. I am not a ghost. I swear to you, it's me. It's Mary. We're lovers. Don't you remember? Please say that you remember me." She forced his hand to her face. She could feel the scars pressing against her cheek, what years of hard work and misery had done to such beautiful, strong instruments. She stared at him, and at first he looked away.

"Please leave me," he said.

"Look at me again," she begged. "One last time."

He turned his face toward her. She could see with perfect vision now. Winter's chill could not make her blink. The sadness swelling in her eyes could not make her blink. She was fixed, in this spot, in this moment. She was home.

"Forgive me, Joshua," she cried, watching her fragile breath escape. "I didn't know. I didn't see before. I swear."

"I told you, pretty, pretty," Lucas gloated. "You belong to me." His wings climbed out of his spine, the edges of them red and black. He showed his true form and stepped closer to possess her. "Sorry to wake you, old friend," he mocked.

"Seasons change. You will suffer for this, Lucas! I swear it. You will suffer."

The trees stirred around them. The wailing that Mary had heard roar through her being when she flew here returned. If trees could feel, they were dying. If the wind had a soul, it was being torn.

Lucas's eyes flashed.

"Joshua, don't leave me now," she begged.

"Go home."

"I am home. I am. Forever. Oh, the mansion looks so beautiful. You finally finished it, my love. You finished it."

"Yes," came Joshua's solemn reply.

The tears came like a flood. Her words were shaped by a blood-curdling confession. "I don't want to go with him. Let me stay with you. I'm sorry. Let me prove my love. I never meant for this. I never meant to hurt you! It wasn't supposed to be this way."

"Yes, it was," Lucas chanted.

"I was confused, Joshua. I was scared." A rush of images crowded her mind. The anger. The disorder. The unforgiveness. The unborn life her weak shell had lost. The pills she had consumed the night of the storm, when she became reckless behind the wheel. "I can be better. I can love you the way you've always loved me. Let this world burn. I need *you*, Joshua! I know that now. I will love only you. Please, just let me stay with you. Please!"

"Come with me," Lucas snarled. He grabbed her arm, and when he did, his grip singed her skin. Her wing swung around and slapped his jaw. The bat uttered a curse with gritted teeth.

Joshua drew closer, noticing her bloodstained womb. His fingers spread out as if he were going to touch her, but he didn't. "You *have* changed, Mary. I look at you and see...something else. Your skin has changed. Your eyes have a new color, your hands and feet are like that of a crow. How did you get so lost, my love? A widow you've become. I don't know this Mary."

"You do know me! Take me back." Her sobs drowned out the noise around them. "I was wrong. I'm sorry. Please! You still love me, don't you?"

Only silence.

"Enough of this!" the bat seethed. "You are mine, Mary."

"I forgot who I was. I forgot you, Joshua. My home. I didn't know it would be this way. If I knew, I never would've left. Can't you forgive me?"

Joshua sighed and blankly stared.

She reached out to touch him, only this time, she noticed her hand begin to fade. Her wrist reached past his chest, through him. She pulled it back, watching the color peel from her fingertips until eventually, her hand disappeared.

"What's happening to me? What did you do to me, Lucas? What in the world did you do to me!"

"It's been three years, Mary," Joshua said calmly, "since you died."

"What are you talking about?"

"Your little fall, remember?" Lucas said, beaming.

"But you came and healed me. With your magic. You healed me."

"Did he?" Joshua asked.

She felt her bones breaking, her neck falling out of place. She collapsed on her knees, hearing a crunching sound. The pain revisited every joint. "It can't be," she cried. "I am alive."

"I have lived without you for so long, my love," Joshua said.

Mary wanted to bring Joshua closer. She wanted to kiss his lips again. "I did not die!"

"Yes," Lucas said, breathing over her. "You did."

Joshua reached for the creature's hairy, wet throat. "Shut your vile mouth, or I'll cut out your tongue."

"You clearly underestimate me!" Lucas thrust his talon into Joshua's side. A blood-soaked hook slid out seconds later. "Yes, that's it. Feel the torment of everything you love, everything you want, being ripped away from you."

Joshua released Lucas from his grip and hugged his stomach.

Mary screamed in panic. "He's a beast, Joshua! Don't let him take me!"

Joshua was still.

Mary's ruined dress began to vanish as well. She could feel the wing pulling at the muscles and bones in her back. It touched Joshua. It was the only part of her that could. She looked behind her and took in what would be her final sight. The tree. Lucas's ugly shadow encompassed it, but underneath that black shape, she saw a word carved into the bark. The word hadn't changed. *Once.* "It was us, wasn't it? All this time, I was so lost. I didn't know." She gasped. "I didn't know."

"You were my bride," Joshua gasped.

"Forever," she said, watching a tear slip off her face and drip into the snow. "I love you, Joshua. Please forgive me."

The rest of her body began to disintegrate. In seconds, she

could no longer feel anything but the icy winter air making a coffin for the ghost she now was. Her wing lost all its feathers, turned ugly, withered.

Lucas exhaled deeply. She appeared again but with no real shape. Mary was a haunting, pale apparition, imprisoned by a black wedding dress. Its material was wrinkled, had cuts in it. Her knotted hair hung across scrawny, malnourished shoulders. The wings remained in this new indistinct shape.

"Quite a wonder, isn't she?" Lucas said to Joshua.

"Leave me, you menace," Joshua said, gazing up at the beast from his knees. He could barely inhale. "I can't...bear to look at...her like this."

Mary stood speechless. She could only stare at Joshua with eyes that were less than human. Lost eyes. Sad eyes. But she would stay in this moment—looking at him, him looking at her—forever, if she could.

Lucas pulled Mary's ghost closer, possessing her. Then, kneeling down into the earth, he gathered his strength and leapt, soaring into the sky with powerful force.

8

JOSHUA WAS ALONE FOR A long while. The wind stirred around him, moving the trees to his right and left. He lay on his back, studying the dark winter sky, how his breath dissipated into the black. Minutes felt like hours. His eyes drifted to the wound in his side. The opening bled out, and every time he quivered, he lost oxygen. But he couldn't accept this terrible end. He wouldn't.

Joshua stumbled to his feet, taking in the beauty of the mansion. In a blink, he remembered the countless hours he spent toiling and working hard to perfect the home. The mansion was complete at last.

But he had not fought so hard to keep it all intact if Mary could not be among its beauty.

He wanted her soul here. It wasn't right that she was gone. That she had been stolen from him. He could make it right again, couldn't he?

She's dead, his mind whispered. *She's dead*.

In the far back of the property, there existed a stone house. It was small, little more than a garage. A sepulcher. He wandered to its path, which was hidden from anyone who did not know its way. The wind sifted through his hair, chilling his scalp and his bones. He shivered as he gazed upon stone. The symbols carved into the top and sides of the structure meant just as much now as they did when he had them carved three years ago. On the left was the symbol for beginning. On the far right, a symbol for end. In the center, there existed a solitary symbol unlike the other two. Eternity.

Joshua felt a burning in his lungs every time he breathed. But he would not stop. He walked toward the door and pressed his dry lips against it. Using a key from his pocket, Joshua unlocked the sepulcher. A white mist seeped out into the snow, causing a new group of flowers to spring to life.

He stepped inside. The sound of his footsteps seemed to echo, despite the fact it was such a small enclosure. Perfect and imperfect stones made up the walls and roof. A small hole existed at the top, which let a pencil-thin light inside.

He wept, thinking of all of the memories he had not yet shared with Mary. It could not end this way. It would not end this way. He uttered her name. The trees outside the stone walls seemed to cry as he spoke. He rubbed his hands together, the scars and cuts he'd endured over the years on each palm touching. "Mary," he uttered again.

She lay so still on a metal bed with flowers and tree bark surrounding her corpse. But it did not look much like a corpse at all. Her skin maintained a milky hue, and not a day of aging had corrupted her. Hair as beautiful as a sunset cascaded down shoulders as young as the day he married her. The power running through the trees had kept her body from wilting. A white rose had been placed in her hands, which were resting softly atop her chest. The wounds from the accident remained, along with the blood stains and torn materials, but beneath it all, Joshua knew his bride was not lost.

"I love you." Joshua wiped his tears and lifted her off the surface. He carried her out of the tomb and across his landscape. The snow did not relent. Lightning ripped across the sky and rain suddenly slipped from heaven. Fog sought to confuse the path, but he knew the way. He would risk what little air remained in his lungs. He had to keep moving.

Joshua fought the cramps adding to the pain of his wound. He inhaled the gray smoke of the world, the reality of her fall. The night was a black mask trying to choke every hope from his throat. He didn't care. He could smell the age of the earth in his nostrils; it smelled broken.

He didn't know how long he'd been walking, carrying his love in his arms, but finally he stopped. A bolt of lightning lit the darkened sky. Thunder grumbled in the distance soon after. His heartbeat jolted. The rain dripped into every particle of snow, melting, melting. Joshua could still see the tracks from the tires of Mary's vehicle, where she'd lost control three years earlier. The guardrail had been replaced, but in his mind, he pictured the former one, twisted and destroyed. He could almost hear the sound of the collision, feel her panic as glass from the windshield showered over her.

"Mary," he whispered once more, the thoughts starting to die. She didn't move in his arms. She lay in silence. Since he had removed her from the table, her skin had begun to deteriorate. This was the spot. At last reached. He knew it perfectly. Often he would come here, experience her pain again and again. Some would call him sick, but it wasn't a sickness. It was a love deeper than the ocean.

"Forever," he finally whispered, falling to his knees. His bones ached upon impact with the slick pavement. Joshua started wheezing. He continued to lose breath fast. But the stinging in his ribcage could not stifle his love.

The road became quiet, except for the cooing of the haunting trees. They too wanted the chance to be human. Such tragic creations they were, left to exist in lonely unity within these woods.

"Lucas!" Joshua screamed at the top of his voice, cradling Mary against his chest.

His eyes roamed the dark. Another bolt of lightning divided the sky. He waited. The very name of that sadistic creature put vengeful thoughts in him. He wished to tear those fangs from his mouth, to shred each wing and crush that arrogant windpipe that bred curse upon curse.

"Lucas!" he howled again. Blood drained from his side every time he spoke, every time he moved. He brought Mary's neck upward, kissing her hair. New lines spread across her cheeks as seconds turned to minutes. Black veins and new blood. "Forever," he whispered into her.

Time ceased.

He groaned.

And then the sound of wings disturbed the air.

The beast descended from the sky. "Well, well. I thought I smelled your weak blood. Long time, no see. What do you want, Joshua?"

Drops of rain clung to the ends of Joshua's hair. He turned to face his enemy. "You deceived her."

"I gave Mary what she wanted."

"What she *thought* she wanted," Joshua corrected.

"She was lost long before she ran to me."

"You put her inside of a nightmare. Your world...is...a disguise, a frail replica. You could never love her...like I did. Like I still do."

"Suddenly a change of heart. This is quite a different song than what I heard earlier."

Joshua's stare drilled the beast.

"You know, I still get excited over human meat. Do you know why?" A pause. "Because of choice. It's their choices that make 'em vulnerable."

"And beautiful."

"That's what you still see?" Lucas growled. "Are you blind? That's her corpse in your arms, yet still you pathetically believe in a love that no longer exists."

Joshua struggled for breath. "You are a liar! All you know... is ruin."

The beast showed his fangs; they dripped red. "Spare me the dramatics, architect! My strengths are growing, as you've seen. Your father has left these woods behind. He has departed, and in doing so, left their future to me. I've been busy since you've been away. Do you really think you can just return and all will be as it once was?"

"My family's power is still strong in this place. You're...just a passing shadow here."

Lucas seethed, exposing his wings again. "Do not waste my time! Why did you call me here?"

Joshua pressed his temple against Mary's chest then raised his head once more. "Give her soul back."

Lucas roared with amusement. "Sorry, but precious belongs to me now. Fair is fair."

Joshua retrieved the utility blade from his pocket and cut his wrist. Blood leaked from the incision. The thick, crimson stream seduced the creature.

"You tempt me with your blood?"

"I came here to make a deal."

"Really?" A long plume of smoke escaped the creature's extended snout. "Pray tell the details."

Joshua blinked then said, "Return Mary. You can have me in her place."

"Do you take me for a fool? No one has ever tasted your blood."

"You will. I mean...what...I say. Let her go, and take me instead."

Lucas folded his wings and became a man again. "Ah, so there's the catch. Return your bride and get the mere corpse of her savior."

"My blood runs through these veins. My family's blood. You've lusted after it...since we built the mansion here."

Lucas's tongue slithered out.

"Taste it, if you doubt me."

Lucas sank his fangs into Joshua's wrist and drank for a long moment. Power escaped.

"Enough," the tired husband heaved. "You have tasted... and seen my commitment to her. Let her go!"

"If you do this, she will live. But you will never see her again," Lucas said, wiping his jaw with his sleeve.

"Not with these eyes."

Lucas salivated. He twitched his neck, impatient and aggravated. "What if I refuse? What if I kill you now and devour your corpse right here just for sport?"

"You can try."

A growl stirred the air around Lucas's nostrils. "If I had my way, I'd watch you ruin, here, where she died. I would make you watch it again and again and again."

A wind sifted through the trees, and Joshua's eyes read frustration. "Release my bride now, or the deal is off."

Lucas scratched at his throat and hesitated before speaking. "So be it, architect. I'll give you what you want." He knelt down beside Joshua and sniffed a strand of Mary's hair. "But know that your torment is coming. It will not be swift. It will not be easy. Every breath will be a new chance for you to suffer. And for you, dear friend, it won't be a dream. It will be a real, living hell. I will take pleasure in seeing you cast down, like a plague. You will humble yourself before me and beg for this world before the end."

Joshua held out his hand, and Lucas dragged his fangs through his wrist once more to finalize the contract. A jolt of energy tore out of Joshua's veins. "It is done, then," he gasped.

With a blink, Lucas shifted into his true form, and Mary's eyes suddenly opened.

"Joshua?" she said, coming to with a soft breath. Her bones shifted into place, adjusting to her body once more. The spots of ruin and hideous wire veins vanished immediately. The healing process had begun.

He kissed her mouth.

"How?" she asked, wide-eyed with amazement.

"They all have a price they're willing to pay," Lucas whispered.

"Him?" Mary said, just noticing the bat's presence. She clung to her lover. "What is he doing here?"

"Your husband and I have an arrangement, darling. Isn't that right, Joshua?"

Joshua nodded.

"No, tell me it's not true."

"You are alive again, Mary. That's all that matters."

"What have you done?"

"I love you. I couldn't...abandon you. I couldn't."

Mary leaned up, breathless. "What will happen now?"

He became weaker by the minute. "Don't be afraid. Just remember. Remember my love for you."

"What will become of you?" she asked, stroking his cheek with her palm.

"I have to go away. It's the way it has to be." Joshua moved closer and whispered into her ear. "But this is not the end. I will see you again...when winter is no more."

She kissed him passionately, and he embraced her lips, her body. Never before had he tasted so much desire.

"It's time for me to go."

"Yes, I'm afraid so," Lucas seethed. "I plan to get creative with you."

Joshua and Mary stood to their feet. He held her in his arms one last time.

"I'm sorry," she cried.

Joshua kissed her cheek. "No more tears." Then, turning to his enemy, he said, "Finish it."

"Gladly." Lucas drove his talon through Joshua's chest and

squeezed his heart until it beat no more. The architect fell limply into his grasp. Lucas smiled a wicked smile at Joshua's bride. "Don't worry. I'll be merciful with what's left." He clutched Joshua's corpse tightly, and leapt into the darkness.

9

MARY'S PULSE REMAINED ERRATIC. She couldn't re-
move the confusion and sadness from her heart. The only man
who had ever truly loved her was gone. But the hope of his
words still lived inside her. She could not comprehend them.
She could not embrace them fully. But she believed.

"Joshua." Saying his name filled her with longing. She
knew he wasn't here. She knew it was her fault he was dead.
Nevertheless, his name was peace, and Mary loved the way his
name flowed from her lips.

She reached the mansion's property. Her feet bore blisters
and cuts. Her sore ankles shot new affliction up each one of
her shins. But she was thankful to feel them at all. She filled
her lungs with air. It was a miracle. It had taken the blood of
true love to save her.

The willow tree at the center of the front yard began to die.
Several of its branches lay scattered and broken at its trunk.
The tree appeared like a sick child, made skinny by malnour-
ishment, left empty and forgotten. Never had she witnessed
beauty quite like it. What a marvel it was to see every other

166 | ESTEVAN VEGA

natural life around it appear so perfectly alive in comparison. The letters carved into its heart had already faded.

Joshua's choice had changed everything.

The snow melted around her feet. She was home, for the last time. A new, innocent breath hung in the air around her, a mystery. Spring was close. So close.

Mary watched with a half-smile as another layer of bark peeled off the willow tree and withered in the dirt. It was then that she felt the bones in her spine shift out of place. Something moved beneath her milky skin, and she winced when she noticed her arms blending colors. She didn't know how long she'd be able to keep the movement controlled, how long she could subdue those mutinous, creeping wings, but as long as she thought of Joshua—of his love....

She turned away from the tree. It would die soon. She was sure of that.

"I will see you again, my love," Mary whispered before her mind could lead her. She walked into the mansion, alone, and closed the door behind her. "When winter is no more."

I HOPE YOU ENJOYED WINTER SPARROW.

Countless hours were spent producing it and promoting it. But there are still readers out there who haven't heard of my work. This is where you come in. The best way to gain new hardcore fans is with the help of existing fans. Please leave a review and help spread the word about *Winter Sparrow*.

BE A PART OF THE MOVEMENT. BE A PART OF THE STORY.

AND NOW, A PREVIEW FROM

ARSON

BOOK ONE IN THE ARSON SAGA

CHAPTER ONE

THE LAKE WAS QUIET.

A lazy fog hovered over the surface of the grey water, whispering in the wake of currents and steady ripples. The world seemed dead to Arson Gable, silent anyway. Like the calm before a storm.

It waited.

Arson stepped off the porch onto the lawn; his mind was swimming. This was where he came most mornings while Grandma slept. He cut his gaze toward the lake, a black womb that rested beyond and beneath the rickety dock. It was as if the lake knew his name and his heartbeats, much like the streets and corners of this town knew his name, cold and faceless as they were. Whether or not he wanted to admit it, this place was home, and there was no going back.

A bright light burned in the sky far off. The distant ember glow was still somehow blinding. Arson breathed deeply and blinked, welcoming the dark rush of black behind his eyelids. When he opened them again, he could see the towering oaks rooted deep in the ground. Their thick branches stretched upward into the clouds, some parts draping over the shady spots of the worn-out cabin. One final glance and he was reminded that these tortuous, beaten things seemed to swallow the world. Just thinking about them—how he'd watched them ruin—made him seem small, so worthless.

Arson made a fist and felt the heat swell in his grip. He wanted to run into the brush, to get lost deep in the small section of backwoods Grandma had forced him to avoid ever since they'd moved here. But he didn't move.

This town seemed so close-knit and yet so separated. Less than a mile up the road were a country market, restaurants, and a bowling alley. There was even a liquor store, a cheap pharmacy, and some fast-food chains, and a few miles past that, a movie theater and a nightclub. But at the heart of this place was disunity, a fierce and futile fight to be known and accepted. Arson never understood why Grandpa had picked here to have the cabin built, right beside the lake.

As Arson slowly approached the dock, his mind returned to thoughts of Danny, the only childhood friend he'd ever had. Dim mornings somehow made each memory more real, hard to let go and even harder to erase. Was he always here, always watching? Odd how seven years could come and go without warning, as if the world blinked and somehow forgot to open its eyes again.

In all fairness, it had never been his grandparents' intention to stay anywhere for too long, but it seemed East Hampton, Connecticut, had become a part of them now, a part of him. "One day we'll be like the rest of them," he recalled Grandpa saying—a man of ideals, empty dreams, and hopes Arson could never freely call his own.

Eventually, they had grown tired of running. This dull corner of the world seemed ordinary enough for them to believe starting over again as normal folks would be possible. "Forget what happened all those years ago in Cambridge," Grandma said so many times that Arson imagined her screaming it to him while he slept. But it was always there— the memory—a splinter in the back of his mind. No going back. Ever.

Arson staggered across the dock, images of child play and stupid laughter pouring in all at once. Danny's face stuck out the most, and behind that he glimpsed their old home in Cambridge and flashes of his first birthday. His mother wasn't there, though, nor dear old Dad, but that day had been recounted to him only once by his grandfather, and it stuck.

Nevertheless, with every joyous memory, distilled regret was close behind. He sometimes imagined what it might be like to get thrown in jail by some nameless special agent and be forgotten, or to wake up and find strong hands squeezing the life out of him.

Arson was an unusual boy. A freak. He knew it. And he hated it. Whatever lingered inside his bones always left as quickly as it came, breathing out in short moments of fear or rage. Over the years, he'd asked to be examined to locate the source of his imperfection and if possible terminate it. After all, why did he sometimes wake up in the middle of the night with a fever? How come his sweat sizzled when it hit the ground? What was he?

Grandma always argued there wasn't much point in talking to no-good doctors or even finding out answers to questions he was better off not asking in the first place. Some people were just born with demons, she'd say.

Arson swallowed hard and threw a stone into the water. The splash shattered his reflection, and ripples spread across the dark surface. He wondered why he was the way he was, wondered why those little girl's parents quit looking all of a sudden, why the investigation against two stupid boys evaporated. Perhaps they didn't care about retribution, or maybe they were just sick of chasing shadows.

I want to be free, Arson thought, nausea creeping up into his gut. While boats raced along the surface of the lake, Arson stared in awe. They vanished so easily, like mist gliding across the water and dissolving into nothingness. What if men could do the same? There was a man once, he'd heard, who walked upon water and didn't sink. Maybe he could too. Maybe one day there would be those who believed in him.

Arson's gaze moved over the lake, across to the other side, where Mandy Kimball lived, and her neighbor, his science teacher from the ninth grade. Then his eyes drew back to the ripples spread out before him, to the dying cabin behind him, as he spit. Beads of sweat streamed down his bony frame, his ash-brown hair trapped inside the gritty creases of his forehead. Arson listened for the lake's soothing melody but couldn't hear it. He focused instead on the sound his feet made atop the splintering dock, kind of like the way swings sounded in cheap horror flicks—empty, rocking back and forth to no melody at all. Closer to the edge he came, lingering.

With shut eyes, he stepped out onto the water and began to sink. Peace soon abandoned him to the lake's shallow world. In a blink, he was looking through the eyes of a ten-year-old boy.

"I don't like fire," he heard the boy say, so frightened, so naïve. "It's dangerous."

"Don't be such a wimp," came his older friend's taunts. "Just light it already."

With each shove and curse, the memory turned alive; it was as if it knew he was watching and didn't like it. The pain still stung, images wilting and dying, only to come alive again and again.

I. Hate. Fire.

Arson could feel the cold, could even remember the way everything sounded or how there was no sound at all. Until the night shattered. The weight of remembering dragged him down while he sucked in a filthy drag of water, his coffined body jerking. The veins on his head began to swell. He was choking.

Time to return to the real world, to release the nightmare once more into the dark of the lake. The struggle eventually pulled him to the surface. Slinging his head back and forth, Arson fought to bring himself out of the bitter current, eventually falling upon dead grass. He tasted the grit of sandy dirt in his teeth. Panting, Arson stood up slowly and staggered toward the cabin, where Grandma Kay's shadow guided him in.

There was something strange that came over Grandma when she exacted punishment, like a part of her enjoyed it too much. She said fixing their leaky roof was a good and righteous way of killing the demons inside him. Nothing like hard work. She said there was no way a lake could cleanse a boy's troubled mind anyway and that he was just plain stupid for thinking it could. To ease his frustration, Arson let himself believe that if he had been caught any other day, her scorn might have resulted in worse than fixing a leaky roof, which Arson would've had to do eventually anyway.

Grandma's reasons for why she did things, why she treated him a certain way, seemed to get worse with time. It was no secret that she loathed the idea of him diving into the lake, especially if fully clothed. She even claimed there were toxins in the water from pollution that had supposedly killed a bunch of fish years back. But maybe it was a fair trade. He'd returned to the lake all the toxins he'd soaked up with every vile thought. When considered, Grandma's logic didn't seem all that twisted. She probably just didn't want him bringing any of that evil back with him, infected or not. She was superstitious, so Arson made a promise he knew he couldn't keep and said it wouldn't happen again.

The muggy June morning caused his palms to sweat. Arson almost lost his grip on the bucket during the climb to the top but regained his balance before losing any supplies. Spiderman would have been proud. Reading comic books all his life came in handy now and then.

Grandpa took care of the cabin to the best of his ability, had even showed Arson how to repair the roof years back. "If you want something done right, you gotta do it yourself," he recalled. But in spite of his grandfather's hard work, it was clear that time eventually wore away all things, even hope.

Arson worked for about an hour before carelessness got the best of him. A loose, jagged shingle sliced through the palm of his hand. Blood gushed from the wound and onto his leg. He swore as the sting began to overwhelm him. He chucked the hammer and tried to keep pressure on the cut.

"What happened?" Grandma's voice echoed from below. "I heard you cussin' all the way in the kitchen. You know how I feel about that."

"Sorry, Grandma." Arson was glad she left it at that. Sitting on the roof, he turned slightly toward the sun. *It's a gusher*, he thought. Then, as he stared in amazement, he watched the wound cauterize itself in seconds. It burned.

"Arson, are you all right up there?"

He looked down at the remaining scar, struggling to make sense of it, neglecting the mess on his clothes. "Just fine, Grandma," he called down.

"That roof isn't going to fix itself. If I have to spend another night with drops of water hitting my face, I promise you'll regret it."

"All right," Arson said. "I'll get back to work."

By evening, the task was complete. He braced himself and watched the sunset from the rooftop as it melted against a fluorescent sky. Arson listened as Grandma concluded her tea conversation with the man she loved.

Moments later, their time together ended with laughter, and he knew it was safe to come down. Arson caught her while she was clearing away the silverware and china.

"Did you finis the roof, love?" she asked in a pleasant voice.

"Yes, Grandma. It's healed...I mean, fixed."

"Marvelous. Say, whatcha mean *healed*?"

Arson grabbed the ladder. "I'm really tired. I'm not think-ing straight right now. Maybe I just need some rest."

"I think you're right. You're not making any sense at all. Say, do you want a piece of cake before I put it away? Grandpa didn't eat much tonight. He's never been much for carrot cake."

"No thanks. Not hungry," he said.

"Suit yourself. Put your tools away and get on up to bed, then. A growing boy like you needs his rest. I hope you learned your lesson, though. I don't like you spending so much time in that miserable lake. The very idea doesn't sit well with my soul."

Arson nodded with reluctant eyes and put away the ladder and the tools. Then he rushed inside the cabin and up to his room to read a comic book before dozing off. Maybe tonight his dreams would be different.